And the Wars Went on Without Him

Jeffrey Pacitto

Author's Note

Growing up in the Greater Toronto Area near Willowdale, I was fortunate to have all four of my grandparents living within walking distance of my home. While they all lived through trying times during the wars and through immigration and old age, they never really sat down to tell me stories of their experiences. Whether that reflected their desire to forget, or my own youthful indifference to their tales at the time, it meant I never got to experience their lives through their words.

How then do you find yourself reading a historical fiction about the life and times of two Italian immigrants during the Second World War and beyond? While never sitting me down to tell me their experiences, I garnered snippets of stories as they'd make comments to others, or through ideas and experiences they passed on to their children, my parents' generation. Add to that a healthy helping of my own time with them in their later lives as age caught up with them.

Taking all I had heard, I've distilled it into the stories you are about to read. Make no mistake, they are all fiction. Some names are real names, some events are real events, and some places are real places; however, they are used fictitiously throughout this collection and with a great deal of invention in places.

And of course, as always, any direct resemblances to people living or dead is purely coincidental.

—Jeffrey Pacitto

To my grandparents, who sacrificed everything and took the biggest leap of faith to bring their families to a new world full of hope.

To my parents, who dedicated their lives to giving me every opportunity to be who I wanted to be.

And to my wife and kids, who inspire me every day to chase my dreams.

Without all of you, I couldn't be who I am.

—Jeffrey Pacitto, 2020

Contents

Living in the Shadow

1. Thursday, August 22, 1918

Angelo's shadow stretched long and faint, wavering across the field, and betrayed his spindly three-foot form. His arms outstretched, they formed crescent arcs across the grass, swiping through the air. He breathed deeply, his tiny square chest rising and falling, ribcage expanding and collapsing in smooth, deep swells. Immersed in his own world, the burbling of the creek was distant, hollow, echoing down the tunnel of his mind, miles away. The gentle wind whistled through the sparse line of pines running to his left towards the creek, spiraling down that tunnel, along with the attenuated voice of his mother, calling out for him from behind. His eyes moved slowly, opening and closing, blinking at the speed of a slow shutter camera, and a smile began to broaden across his soft, olive skin.

"Angelo!"

Her voice faded in, invading his reality, collapsing the tunnel of his mind into itself, turning the shadow-scythe reaper into nothing but an effigy of an adolescent boy, swaying with the grass in the ever-weary Mediterranean sun.

"Veni qui!" she called in a quick staccato beat.

Her right hand hung by her side, bony index finger pointing down to her feet, knobby knuckles swollen against taught skin. Her ever-present white apron flapped across her arm in the warm breeze that hummed against the whistle of the trees. Her bare feet stood solid on the smoothed stone landing. She was a resolute statue, her cracked dry heels blending into the crevasses in the cobbles.

Angelo's eyes remained gently shut, squeezing every last moment he could out of the fantasy he was enjoying as he spun around on his own tattered heels to face his mother. The upturned corners of his mouth dropped slowly as he opened his eyes, leaving his imagination behind. Stepping forward into a jog, he reached deep into the pocket of homemade burlap trousers that dropped to a ragged hem just below his knee and grabbed hold of a cool, brass bullet he'd found two days earlier on the side of the road near one of the neighbouring fields. Not just a casing either, an actual bullet. He held it in his palm in that pocket, turning it over and over again, feeling the smooth slickness of it as he ran, his free arm swinging wildly. He worried it would slip out as he ran, and he couldn't bear the thought of being separated from his treasure.

The sun flickered through the trees that lined the Southern Apennines to the east, stabbing at the periphery of his sight. His eyes twitched ever so slightly with each bright spear piercing into the edge of his vision. Angelo's mother flickered in and out of darkness, like Maria Caserini at the picture house, as the sharp beams intermittently blinded him and haloed his mother.

Their family home sat low to the ground. Originally built by his great grandfather, each stone laid by his large strong hands, one upon the next, building a fortress for his family for generations to come. Two square rooms, fifteen feet on each side, divided by a wall of hand-hewn stone, comprised the total area of the house and provided scarcely enough space for Dominic and Alessandra's three children.

The lush fields of crops and grass tapered off as they approached the house, surrounded as it was by a moat of dark, hard packed soil, hammered by years of footfalls as children and parents alike worked and played about its foundations. An outdoor oven constructed of similar stone sat apart from the home and wafted a fine tendril of sweet acrid smoke into the air from its mortar gnarled chimney.

To the right of the building lay a fenced-in area, half-covered by planks of rotted oak, the wood grain etched and weathered by the decades. The family cow, sectioned off from the two dozen hens, leaned under this overhang, remaining close to the house, in the relative cool of the shade. The squawking chickens high-stepped around their cage, pecking at the pebbly soil and ruffling their feathers in the late-day sun. To the left, lay a half dozen oak planks bound to two thick crosspieces and weighted down by five heavy stones, and beneath this lay a broad well, a hand-dug convenience Domenic had felt necessary to make his house a home. Alessandra thought him foolish for taking the time to dig such an extravagance, but Domenic insisted.

"In the cold, in the winter, you would have our children walk to the river just to drink!"

Alessandra scoffed, if it was good enough for her to fetch water from the river growing up, it would be good enough for her children as well. Domenic had won that argument, however; and once he started digging, she didn't stop him.

The leaves of the trees murmured their reedy song as a cooler wind swept down from the mountain and bustled through their boughs, spreading itself across the wide plain, drawing a muted hymn from the wheat stalks. Angelo's loose clothing shook in the breeze and he spread his arms wide, leaving the bullet to hang heavy in the pocket of his homemade trousers and allowing the heaven-sent wind to cool him and usher him home.

When he reached the stone stoop, worn smooth from years of traffic, his mother had already gone inside, the wooden door swinging back slowly on rust-dry iron hinges with a rising whine. She had left the lid of the rainwater barrel that flanked one side of the door just off the edge of the stoop slightly ajar, but Angelo took no notice of it. He bounded up the stairs like some demigod climbing the steps of Olympus, or an eager parishioner on Easter at the Chiesa San Benedetto. Turning, he gave one final glance at the waving plains of grass and wheat — the clouds above engaged in the grand waltz of late summer — before stepping across the threshold into the cool dank of his house.

2. Saturday, September 7, 1918

Angelo had been back to school a week and the structure of his days had changed. Gone was his free time to bound through the fields and so he sat in the kitchen with his mother. The smooth mottled yellow-grey stone wall ran close to Angelo's back, each block lifted into place generations ago by hands worn worse than even his father's calloused palms. He always thought of those hands as like the bark of the chestnut trees that grew along the edge of the dirt roadway that led to his school.

"Mama, why did they build the monastery on top of the mountain?"

Angelo had his arm stretched over the long dining table in the home's common room, absentmindedly drilling the index finger of his right hand into a small smooth knot in the wood. His frame was dwarfed by the giant seat his father had built, his shoulders cresting just over halfway up the gently curved back of the chair. His right arm had to arch in a curve to reach the tabletop, while his left remained draped lifeless by his side, resting palm-up on the hard, flat seat of the chair.

Alessandra stood hunched over at the counter, her shoulders rolling forward and back as her hands worked. She wore a flower-print smock, one of three virtually identical wool outfits she owned, covered in the front by the ever-present white apron. She periodically wiped her hands on the rough fabric as she kneaded dough against the polished concrete counter.

"I've told you before, Angelo," she said, and her hands reached for her apron once more, fingers spread wide, wiping them in long controlled strokes against the thin cotton, both palms and backs. "So that they could be closer to God."

Angelo demurred, continuing to admire the futility of his tiny finger drilling incessantly against the reddish black-brown wood. His eyes unfocused, staring beyond his fidgeting finger as his mother's hands returned to the powdered dough, her knuckles pressing it into submission, her fingers disappearing into its bulbous mass.

"I know," he said. "I just wanted to make sure."

He paused for a moment, unintentionally. His finger stopped drilling, his body still, as if the churning of his thoughts could expend no other energy to fire commands to the rest of his body while it worked. His words began slow, coming in languid chops.

"Vincenzo says that they had to build it there so they could stop running from people," he said, "and keep an eye on them." His eyes flashed to his mother, staring intently at the twisted brown hair knotted in a bun at the back of her bobbing head. "And to fight them if they had to."

His body remained still, staring at his mother, an unexpected calm in the energized body of youth. His mother's hands had stopped their mechanical grind. Her shoulders followed suit, ceasing to roll moments later, and her head gave one final bob. Her body reacted from the furthest tips of her extremities to her core. Her hands didn't move to her apron, but instead sat on the counter. Her head dropped slightly, her strong shoulders losing their tension and slacking weakly as a silent breath exhaled long from her concave chest.

"Sometimes," she said. "Perhaps."

Her eyes closed, head cocking slightly side to side. She paused with intention, thinking of how best to answer her eight-year-old's question, as deeply probing as it was without his realization. She nodded.

"Yes. Yes, they have to watch people, sometimes, and make sure they're all doing God's work." She cracked a half smile to herself, creasing new age into the smooth, hard features of her face. "Doing God's work well."

Her hands began their work again, fingers more gingerly massaging into the dough as her shoulders began to roll again and her back straightened, a new-found joviality to her task.

Angelo's head tilted to the left as he thought.

"Because Vincenzo says that people can't speak to God, so no one knows if they're doing God's work or not."

His finger was about to begin its twisting pilgrimage into the knot of wood again, but after a side-glanced moment of contemplation, he moved his hand down to his side with a slight shrug and gripped the edges of the seat. He began swinging his dirty bare feet, his right foot out of sync with his left.

Alessandra paused again, her body freezing this time, hands splayed on the counter, palms down like before. Suddenly jerking back into motion, her hands slipped down to the front of her apron, wiping them in quick short bursts against the weak coarse fabric.

"This is Vincenzo, Gena's boy?" she asked, a little more ire in her voice than she intended. Her head inclined ever so slightly upwards and to the right, eyes stretching backwards in Angelo's direction.

"Yes," he said.

His body straightened in his chair, eyebrows darting upwards. His legs slowed their swinging momentum and then resumed their pace when his mother didn't respond. The bread began to take shape again in the womb of her hands as her shoulders rolled once more, thumbs caressing the pale flesh of the dough as she cupped it gently, coaxing it to form. All the while her mind recalled the last dozen Sunday masses and recent confessions and encounters with the church, contemplating how Father Masella would respond to such an innocent transgression.

"His mother prays," she said in slow, measured tones, "every Sunday at church for her husband." The conviction in her voice grew as she found the right words, as if spoken *through* her, not by her. "And she says God sends her messages that he's okay."

Pleased with herself, she continued with even more confidence in her voice, channeling Father Masella and the candour of the passionate sermons he brought to his flock.

"People don't talk to God like I'm talking to you now, Angelo." She raised a doughed hand and gestured it back and forth between her and the stone wall in front of her, her fingers flapping like the tail of a lethargic fish. "They talk in feelings."

Her hand hovered in the air, touching her breastbone, tapping her heart. Her head, cocked at an angle that let Angelo see just the corner of her right eye, flicked almost imperceptibly, enforcing the validity of her claims while simultaneously encouraging his agreement. Her eyes slid back to the dough before her as her emoting hand ramped back up into motion, plunging her calloused thin knobby red fingers back into the sticky powdered lump of dough.

Angelo's head tilted to the right as he thought.

"No," he said, "that's not what Vincenzo means."

His legs swung fervently, and his right arm beginning to snake a secretive path back to the top of the table, one finger outstretched to prod at the smooth, dark knot there again.

"He means that people can't talk to God because God doesn't exist."

Angelo's finger had found purchase, but just as it had, his mother spun around, twisted awkwardly, painfully even, at the hips so her entire upper body faced Angelo. Her lower limbs caught up to her sudden snap turn as her eyes whitened, soft hazel pupils dilating to a violent green. Her eyebrows arched like devil sticks across her brow and the scent of sulfur was nearly palpable as her tongue flamed out of her thin, pale, parting lips. Dough on her hand flew off in tiny dollops as an accusing finger shook in Angelo's direction, her gaze flitting between his head and his heart—at a loss as to which to blame.

Her voice stabbed at him, sharp and forceful.

"Out. Now."

Angelo's eyes were wide. He blinked helplessly as he slid slowly from the seat and slunk towards the adjacent room. Halfway to the yawning arch, his mother called after him.

"And you had better ask God to forgive you for what you said."

She had a way of sounding forceful, but not angry, and loud without yelling. As he crossed the threshold between these two suddenly very different rooms of the house, his mother's words chased after him.

"And pray for Vincenzo, and his mother and father, that God may forgive Vincenzo and keep them all safe and well!"

The room fell silent around Alessandra, and in the stillness, she could feel her heart pounding in her chest. She closed her eyes, her mind scanning the room, placing everything in perfect order as was expected, as was right, as she turned from the dark recess of the opening between rooms, between worlds, to the firmament of the counter, covered in flour and piles of semi-formed dough.

Facing the counter, her hands tensed inches above its worn surface. She opened her eyes, her lips parting ever so slightly as she let out a sigh, releasing the tension that held her entire body in seizure. Her hands fell to the countertop, kicking up tiny plumes of flour, like a soldier's footfalls on a sun-parched battlefield, and she huffed at a few loose strands of hair that had fallen across her face. Resting her weight, and the weight of her family, on her left hand, her right hand crossed her body, wrist limp, as she called out the holy trinity in her thoughts and asked for forgiveness.

The stubborn strands of hair that had fallen from the long braid tightly wrapped about her head swayed before her eyes again, and with another huff at them, she leaned back into her work with much less enthusiasm, more mechanical necessity, as the wide sagging spheres of dough to her right fermented on the counter.

3. Monday, September 9, 1918

Angelo's step had a slight spring in it as he kicked stones along the dusty path on the side of the road. Tiny clouds chased the pebbles as he booted them along, leading him to school. The day was warm—the sun already high enough to break a dirty sweat across his smooth, young brow. His meagre collection of books hung low to the ground, strapped together with an old spalled strip of bridle leather his father used to use to yoke the cow when it came time to plow the fields. Angelo's older brothers had commandeered it to strap a small wooden cart to the family dog so they could help bring vegetables to the market when there were spare vegetables to sell. The strap felt experienced to Angelo, like it had experienced more than he could ever hope to, each crackling vein in the dark exterior revealing a creased wrinkle of wisdom.

As he made his way up the slight incline of the road, he raised his head, and a small bead of sweat raced down his small, slightly upturned nose, where it beaded at the end and fell off in a tiny drop that saturated a spiky circle of dust under his feet. He squinted towards the horizon as the wavering silhouette of Vincenzo crested the hill ahead. Angelo didn't wave, not like he usually did, his right arm remaining glued to his side, his left slowing its joyful saunter, the books at the end of their tether lolled like a swing without a child, as it slowed to match his now less vibrant stride. His eyes returned to the dusty gravel below his feet, and he punted another rock ahead of him, watching as it skipped and hopped along in an erratic zig-zag pattern, eventually ending in a tumble down into the shallow ditch that skirted both sides of the roadway. Looking for another stone, his eyes preceded him and found their way back up to Vincenzo, who was now a great deal closer but still shrouded in an unusual darkness. The sun was more to his left than directly behind him, but he strode in feigned relief.

As the distance between them closed, Angelo's eyes couldn't look away from his friend, and he began to make out Vincenzo's distinctive features—his thin, sharp jawline, sunken red cheeks, oversized ears, and thick tapered eyebrows that always seemed to move with a will all their own. Today his eyebrows appeared to match his scowl, angled deep over the cavities of his pale green eyes, those eyes staring daggers at Angelo. Even from fifteen paces away, he could clearly see that. He could clearly see Vincenzo was not happy today, nor was he trying to hide that fact. The arch of his shoulders and slant of his head made that clear enough, not to mention the determined aggression that oozed from every step he took towards Angelo along that beaten path beside the road that led from the farms to the school.

At ten paces, Angelo saw the mottled blue and yellow of a swollen welt above Vincenzo's right eye and the dark rings encircling both eyes, plunging them in perpetual shadow.

"Vincenzo . . ." he said, concerned for his friend.

"Angelo."

Vincenzo grimaced through clenched teeth. His lips puckered into a slight frown, cracking a heretofore unseen split in his lower lip, causing him to wince slightly on the last vowel of Angelo's name.

Dropping his books to the dusty ground, Angelo raised his hands in a compassionate gesture. His mouth opened, but before he could ask what had happened, Vincenzo's body snapped. Like a coiled spring dislodging from the intricate weaving of a pocket watch, he threw aside Angelo's helping hands and pointed an extended finger at the swollen bruise over his eye.

"This?" Vincenzo's eyes were wild. "This is thanks to *you*, y'moron."

"Me? What did I do?" Angelo stammered, his arms half raised, the weight of confusion dropping them slowly to his side. His concerned expression for his friend turned quickly into genuine confusion.

"Why you gotta go and tell your mama everything we talk about, huh?" Vincenzo barked at Angelo. "You go tell her you cut class too?" he asked in a sardonic tone.

"No, I don't . . ." Angelo spoke slowly, each word padded with enough silence to fill a church pew.

"Or that you've smoked cigarettes?" Vincenzo wasn't listening to Angelo. He wasn't done his beratement yet, wasn't clear of his thoughts. His fingers intimated smoking, tapping his index and middle finger against his lips.

"I don't tell her that . . . I . . ." And all at once realization dawned on Angelo.

Vincenzo could see it in his face.

"Yeah, exactly!" Vincenzo spat the words at Angelo. "So now my mama's gonna make me go to church every Sunday with her and pray every night for my papa."

The crack on his lower lip had started bleeding at some point, and a tiny rivulet of blood ran part way down his jutting chin.

"But Vincenzo . . . your mama . . . *she* did this?" Angelo's eyes darted around Vincenzo's face, his young mind trying to process the horrible abuse brought on by the seemingly innocuous questions he had asked his mother, questions he was genuinely interested in finding answers for. He never imagined for a moment the answers would come at the end of a fist.

"No, she used the willow branches." Vincenzo bent, pulling up his pant legs to expose numerous fine cuts across his shins, calves, and the backs of his knees. They were still a fresh raw pink, unscabbed and throbbing. Angelo could feel the sting of each line that crisscrossed Vincenzo's legs, feel the warm pain that followed for hours after.

"I couldn't feel them afterward," said Vincenzo, "and when I tried to walk, I fell and hit my head." He accentuated the incident with a nod of his head, pantomiming the tumble that caused his facial trauma.

"I'm *so* sorry, Vincenzo. I didn't even think about it . . ." Angelo was still agog, aware of his transgression but unable to make sense of the brutal consequences meted out. "I didn't think I said anything that would—"

"That's your problem, Angelo, you don't think."

Caught up in his own frustration, Vincenzo almost didn't even sound angry anymore, just exhausted.

4. Friday, September 13, 1918

The noonday sun stood high in the sky, blazing bright and hot almost straight above Angelo and his cadre of friends. The shadows were cast short and sharp, so the boys sat on a slight decline of short grass that ran down from a squat stone wall on the edge of an abandoned field.

Angelo sat, his knees pulled up tight to his chest, keeping even the edge of his feet out of the crackling rays of light that tormented from above. On his left, Egidio was a mirror, reflecting Angelo's pose like a twinned statue at the entrance to a cathedral. On his right, Vincenzo lay on one arm, sprawled out on the grass, his leg toying with the light as he slid his foot through the grass back and forth. Three other boys, Tomaso, Francesco, and Silvano, friends of Vincenzo's, acquaintances of Angelo's, sat on their haunches beyond Vincenzo, tucking their slightly burlier frames into the scarce shade as well. They all wore their grey woolen school shorts and white button-down shirts, untucked and half unbuttoned, trying to release as much of their own heat into the humid saturated air as they could. Egidio rolled up the cuff of his shorts and shifted to kneeling on one knee. The oldest of the group, he was just large enough to not benefit from the sliver of shade in which the other boys sought sanctuary.

"Zio Joe used to live down the way from us," said Angelo, cutting the thick silence with his muted voice.

Angelo was always told that he should be respectful of his elders, and to make them feel special and important in his life, and not too distant, he should always refer to them as 'aunt' or 'uncle' instead of 'misses' or 'mister' or—may Saint Francis Xavier forgive him—use simply their first names.

"He was sick. Last winter."

Angelo wasn't very good at telling stories or anecdotes or even parables. His voice carried no enthusiasm, his body no emotion, his words no rhythm.

"Very sick."

Vincenzo blew out a deep sigh, curling his lower lip out to channel the air towards his forehead, causing the tuft of dirty blonde hair that rested there to puff up and out, before settling back in more or less the exact same position as it started.

Angelo's gaze remained lost in the field before him, as if accessing his memory of Joe took all his concentration, no mental processes left for physical functions.

"The doctor said he didn't know what to do to help him, and Father Masella said all we could do was pray for him to get better." Angelo paused, probably longer than he should have, relating such a simple narrative. "Zio Joe told us that he'd be better when the weather got better, since it was still very cold and dark out."

Again, he paused, and when he was about to speak again, Vincenzo cut him off.

"Angelo," he said, holding the open palm of his right hand towards him. "You have to tell your story faster, how are we ever going to get to do anything today if you keep talking and talking and talking!"

When he had awoken this morning, Vincenzo had hoped he'd have a chance to go to the market with his friends and scam the old man that sold walnuts out of a couple handfuls of them. They were pretty abundant on the trees that bordered most of the farms around town, but there was a thrill, an excitement, from taking them from the market that got his blood pumping just a little bit faster. Almost as fast as it did when they had seen that soldier.

The first time Vincenzo had convinced Angelo to cut class, they had made their way to the market, hoping to get their hands on a few of those walnuts or, if they were lucky, maybe find a gelatiere looking the wrong way to nick a nice limone they could share. Neither of them was prepared for what they *did* see.

A carabiniere—dressed in full military regalia.

The man wore knee-high patent leather boots, dark as the pit of an olive, with belts that ran across his belly and over his shoulder. The rest of his suit was grey, crisp and sharp where the corners of the shirt tucked into his pants and the seams of his pants gave way to his boots. A short cape that fell no further than his hip draped over his shoulder, obscuring his right arm in mystery. He had a finely trimmed beard that ended in a gentle point and a moustache that had actual waxed tips, which twisted an inch away from his cheeks on either side. His piercing serious gaze was on one of the ladies who sold leather goods, and whatever the soldier had said to her before the boys noticed him must have been hilarious because she was giggling and blushing, her head turned slightly away, her eyes cutting a glance at him coyly. From that moment on, they both knew they wanted to be soldiers, and it became easier and easier to convince Angelo to cut class. With the prospect of encountering another carabiniere, how could he say no? Instead, he was sitting in the shadow of a short wall while Angelo stumbled through another of his unending stories. He gave his friend a hard look.

"Okay, well, he was supposed to come over for Easter lunch," Angelo said, a little quicker this time, careful not to stumble over his words, "like he did every year."

The words snapped out of him in quick bursts now with a longer pause between thoughts. Angelo closed his eyes and leaned his head back, the expression on his face taking him back to that day.

"It was the most beautiful spring day you've ever seen, sunny and warm and everything. But that year, he never came over."

Angelo turned his head slowly side to side ever so slightly, almost feeling that spring sun glisten off his face.

The silence hung in the humid air. Not even the shrill birdsongs that often echoed around the valley split the void the open ending of Angelo's story had left. He opened his eyes and turned his head towards the other boy, darting between their blank, hollow expressions. Their bewilderment was palpable, as they waited for the punchline, for the denouement of his story.

Angelo's lips screwed up into a perturbed frown. They hadn't understood him, and he couldn't figure out why. There was such an obvious meaning to his story, so clear to anyone he thought. He waited another moment, his head poking forward slightly, his eyes trying to pull a response from his peers. Letting out a faint sigh, he filled in the blank all his compatriots were drawing.

"He was better, he got better, when the sun came out."

Vincenzo's squinting eyes let Angelo know his words had done little to lead them down the path of enlightenment.

"God took him to heaven," Angelo said finally. "He made all his sickness go away and took him to heaven."

Satisfied with himself, but still unclear as to why he had to explain something so obvious, Angelo's lips drew into a thin line.

The boys remained frozen momentarily, the full depth of Angelo's story taking time to sink in, and while the other boys' faces softened in contemplative understanding, Vincenzo's eyes narrowed. His nostrils flared slightly as a scowl bloomed on his face.

"That's bullshit, Angelo!" Vincenzo slapped at a small mound of dirt, cascading tiny bits of earth and pebbles across the ground before them. "God didn't do anything. Your zio was old and sick and he died." Crossing his body with both arms, Vincenzo swung them out to either side, slicing through the air with an invisible lid to end the conversation.

Angelo looked aghast. His small chin doubled as his head reeled backwards, his entire body bent into a concave spring.

"But . . . but Father Masella said that on Easter the gates of heaven are open, open for everyone, so he was able to get in very easily, without having to wait or anything!"

Vincenzo's head pecked to either side as he began berating Angelo, his voice condescending and patronizing.

"Father Masella doesn't know what he's talking about." The fingers of Vincenzo's right hand met in a purse shape and shook at Angelo, mocking him. "When was the last time he's said something, or prayed for something, and it came true, huh?"

Vincenzo's eyes drilled into Angelo, whose mouth had fallen agape, his mind racing to keep up with Vincenzo and prepare a defence he didn't know was necessary just moments ago. Angelo's eyes began to shift back and forth as he thought, as he racked his brain to produce an instance, just one, or even a half-truth that could be misconstrued as Father Masella's request for divine intervention materializing on this mortal plane. Without a thought of what to say, a creak of air began vibrating along Angelo's vocal cords before Vincenzo cut him off his question merely part of his enraged diatribe.

"I prayed every day that my papa would be okay. That he would come back home okay." He began to shake, ever so slightly, his outstretched hand that previously pleaded with Angelo's innocence now pointed an accusatory finger at him.

"Every day." He jammed his finger towards Angelo, punctuating each syllable. "Me and mama both."

Vincenzo's palm fell open, his hand now limp at his side, and the rage pent up in his shoulders and neck surrendered to a greater sense of abject failure.

"And God let him die."

Not even the wind dared to make a sound, with the tall grass as its instrument, in the silence. All the boys were statues, frozen by Vincenzo's words.

"If God was listening," he said, "why would he let my father die?"

The other boys all remained silent, unmoving, but Angelo's mind had finally clicked in, and he rose to the occasion, snapping out an answer that not only was unwarranted, but unwanted.

"Father Masella says that sometimes God does stuff we don't ask him to do because he knows what's best and . . ." But Angelo

realized too late how cold and uncaring his answer sounded. "I .
. . I mean it's just that—"

An open palm stung the left side of Angelo's face, and he winced
as the shock from it spread across his cheek. The struck side of
his face began to warm and swell slightly.

"You have a brain in there, Angelo, or what?" Vincenzo pulled
his hand back, cocking his arm for another swing, should it be
necessary to silence Angelo again. "Or do they teach you to be
dumb like that in school now?"

"Hey," said Egidio, "lay off the guy, would you?"

He didn't speak much. Egidio's voice was deep and would
sometimes crack, and everyone would laugh at him, so he kept
quiet most of the time. He didn't keep quiet now. And his voice
didn't crack now.

Vincenzo turned his bubbling volcano of rage on Egidio.

"Why? You never gone to school, what makes you think it's so great?" Vincenzo's hands unconsciously balled into fists, his tiny fingers arching into his palms.

Egidio's thick brows knit above his small, almost beady eyes.

"No, I ain't been t'school." His mouth worked over the words like speaking was foreign to him, like he had to taste each syllable before he could spit it out. "But my little brother Nicola, he goes, so lay off of school, okay?" His back arched slightly, his chest rising and falling with deeper breaths as fixed determination found its way to his face.

Vincenzo grunted.

"I'll lay on whatever I want to lay on, Egidio!" Vincenzo rose ever so slightly, his smaller body straining to dominate the larger boy. "I'll lay on your sister if I want to!"

In an instant they both scrambled to their feet, eyes brazen. Both boys' fists were held white-knuckle tight, their arms akimbo, legs tense and coiled, like mountain lions poised to strike. From their crouched positions, the other three boys began pumping their fists, catcalling for a fight, intrigued by the prospect of breaking the monotonous dog days with some excitement. Angelo sat in stunned silence, processing all that had transpired in such a short time.

Egidio's chest heaved a last large sigh as his hands loosened and his shoulders went slack.

"You know, Vincenzo? You're not worth it." He waved two open palms at him, disregarding the young boy. "You'll never learn. Never grow up. Never understand."

Vincenzo's eyes followed Egidio's hands as they pushed at the air between them, and his hands loosened their grip as well. His fighter's hunch went slack, all the tension, all the energy wound up in his tiny frame drained. His expression dropped, eyebrows softening, his eyes almost sinking backwards. He was at a loss.

Egidio turned and lumbered off in the direction of the creek. Barely two paces into his departure, a pair of arms came flailing about his neck from behind, the right hand gripping the left wrist in a choke hold. Francesco leapt from his haunches and cheered as Tomaso and Silvano clapped encouragingly, the humid heat that kept them motionless before a faint memory.

Egidio span around, his upper body bobbing as his legs stumbled in a jagged circle. The mild centrifugal force lifted Vincenzo's legs into the air and his grip began to slip against the gritty sweat of his forearm. Flung like a sack of flour from a cart to a doorstep, he tumbled into the dirt and rolled over twice before quickly scampering to his feet.

In the cloud of dust he had kicked up, he appeared taller, stronger, more of an imposing threat like the actor Luigi Mele, ready for war. Egidio pointed a threatening finger at Vincenzo, his gaze fixedly staring at the young boy.

"You don't want to do this, Vincenzo," he said, but before he could finish what he was about to say, Vincenzo was running towards him in an unbridled rage.

Letting out an animalistic groan, he threw his right arm in a swinging punch but missed as Egidio weaved to his left. Tumbling off to Egidio's right, Vincenzo's body spun off balance with the force of his entire swing, his flailing left arm coming around and accidentally elbowing Egidio in the ribs before striking the ground again. Vincenzo scampered to his feet in a swirl of dust. Egidio stood, hunched at the waist, coughing and holding his chest. Each wheeze between coughs seemed barely deep enough to supply the fuel needed for the coughing fit that followed.

Vincenzo leapt with a short bark and was upon Egidio in an instant. His hands were a blur as he landed blow after blow on the defenseless boy's hacking face. Angelo's eyes grew wide with each strike of Vincenzo's fists on Egidio's head. Sharp red welts began to form across Egidio's brow as his swollen forehead began to squint his eyes shut. Blood began to dribble and sputter from behind his swelling, cracking lips. Vincenzo was unrelenting, striking Egidio with wallop after wallop across his quickly disfiguring face. Tomaso stopped clapping first, his eyes widening. Francesco followed, slowly sinking down to a squat as Silvano began to whimper.

Angelo continued to stare at the horror that was unfolding before him, his own fists tightening at his sides. With each fresh swollen welt cascading across Egidio's face, Angelo's body was flexing, muscles tensioning, poising to strike.

A gurgle of blood spat from between Egidio's lips as his chest convulsed.

Angelo sprang towards the two combatants like a feral cat. He flailed his arms in a blind rage at Vincenzo and struck a blow to the swollen deep bruise above Vincenzo's left eye. Vincenzo stumbled backwards, clutching at the re-inflamed wound on his head with a blood-soaked right hand. He spoke no words, only a deep, guttural, otherworldly growl escaped the clenched jaws of the beast he had become. He launched himself at Angelo.

Then the pain began, and the crying, and the screaming. And with each strike to Angelo's face, each punch to his belly, Vincenzo asked the same thing.

"Where is God now, Angelo? Where is God now?"

Angelo began to wonder the same thing.

5. Saturday, September 15, 1918

The shadows of the tall pines that flanked the side of the grassy field stretched long and faded in the early morning sun, obscuring Angelo's brothers as they traversed the family field, buckets in hand, their father trailing them with a slight limp. The long, yellow grass heaved in deep breaths as a cool prevailing north wind filled them with life. The tiny brook burbled along, ignorant of the day, carrying its fresh water from unseen mountain springs beyond the monastery that crowned Monte

Cassino through the fields and farms of the pious people of the valley.

The undulating field ran towards the squat stone building, whose handmade wooden door was shuttered tightly against the cooling fall weather. The rain barrel sat nearly empty, and the cow languished in the first rays of a rising Mediterranean sun that cut warmer paths through the crude fencing. The scent of a stoked fire sat sharply on the crisp morning air, a tiny rivulet of blue-grey smoke wafting from the chimney at the centre of the building the only conceit to its birthplace.

Inside the kitchen, sprawled on the family dining table, he could feel nothing. No pain. No anger. Not even the soothing cool of the poppy-and-herb balm his mother reapplied to the welts across his naked body. She moved expertly, like a well-trained phalanx of soldiers might march in perfect formation across uneven terrain, although she was only a mother, trained with nothing but instinct.

It was hard to breathe, each inhalation a wheeze reminiscent of the laboured breathing his grandfather suffered late in his life, and so he took small short gasps of air through his broken nose and between loose teeth through the tiniest slit in his thin, serious lips. His mother spoke to him, as she diligently tended to her child's body as best she could.

She spoke to him of life and love, of church and God. She spoke of the mystery of faith, the miracle of the unborn child growing within her, a new life sparked from nothing, destined to reap the rewards of the Lord. But Angelo did not hear her. His mind was elsewhere.

His mind was on the carabiniere from the market in his fine regalia, his cockeyed smile unaware of the horrors he might one day face and perpetrate. His mind was on the bullet he had found, so beautiful and light in form—and yet so ugly and heavy in function. His mind was on the lifeless husk of Joe, gone forever, alone in the void beyond the black veil. And his mind, heaven help him, was without God.

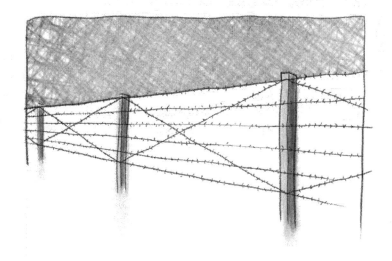

And the Wars Went on Without Him

1. Italy

Carlo

In 1944 Carlo was but a child of six. He had no memories from that time in his life, save for running. He could remember running. Always running. Holding tightly to his mother's salt-worn hands, dry and thick and lined with deep fissures of calloused flesh ... and running. Those hands that had occasionally hit him, punishing him for some now relatively insignificant transgression, presently clung dearly to him, dragging him as she ran to save his life.

His child's mind full of bewilderment, and all he could remember was running. Running and the whistling shriek of the bombs that were chasing them into the cavernous catacombs that snaked their way through the base of the mountain that stretched to heaven. A beacon of solace in a tumultuous sea of despair.

In the relative shelter of the hovels under the great monastery, his mother's heart still raced. His face pressed to her bosom, rivulets of sweat stinging his eyes as they dripped from her skin, he could feel it thumping against this cheek. The whining downpour of bombs was muffled, faint at the end of the tunnel, but each impact shook the earthen walls with such a ferocity it felt as though God himself had the earth in his grasp, shaking it violently. Everything was blurred by a haze of dust as soil rained down all about them. His mother held him tighter yet, her breath coming in sharp heaves, her arms a protective cocoon as the screaming and crying of an entire village of women and children faded away.

By 1945 the war was over. It was the second Great War. The real War to End All Wars. Indeed, it was many things, but mostly it was an end to innocence. Many had died defending both freedom and oppression. Everyone killing in the name of God. Many more had died from disease, the derelict husks of people left by the wayside as forgotten chaff when the bleeding finally stopped and the scars of the world started to knit together. Carlo's father, Angelo, had fought. One of the brave souls forced to take up arms, he was destined to return. His friend Vittorio's father, Giuseppe, had fought too, but he was never to come back. After a while, Vittorio went away, too, and never came back.

When Vittorio left, Carlo was old enough to see how things had changed but not old enough to properly understand why. He could easily see how different their lives were but didn't know why they had to be so different. Vittorio had stopped coming to school after the second year. That summer was the last time he actually played with Carlo in the rare moments they were able to claim for themselves between helping their parents. Vittorio didn't return to school in the fall, he had to help his mother and older brother take care of their house. He had to do things his older brother would have normally done, since his older brother had to do things his father would have normally done. Vittorio could barely take care of himself at school, let alone take care of his whole family. They were only just learning how to read the previous year. Carlo thought about Vittorio nearly every day he sat in class until the end of his fifth year, when all children finished school. In those two years, Carlo finished learning how to read and learned about mathematics and religion. He soon forgot about reading, having no need for it, and only remembered what he needed of mathematics to count crop or, more importantly, gamble.

Their lives had followed such different paths that, when Vittorio finally left Cassino, Carlo had barely noticed. He could remember one of the last times he saw Vittorio. It was a Sunday morning in 1948 while he was on his way to church with his family. Carlo had followed his mother Carmella and father Angelo through their field, the wheat stalks hip-high and swaying slowly in the gentle breeze. They carefully stepped across some protruding stones in the brook that divided their land from that of their neighbours, his mother holding up the hem of her dress, his father reaching back with strong, supportive hands to help them over. They hit the dirt road that snaked away from their tiny plot in the valley and began their trek. They took the slight incline of the road slowly because, although it wasn't steep, it was long and would tire them out should they quicken their pace. As they walked that day, Carlo saw a cart coming down the road towards them. The donkey pulling at the worn cart absentmindedly swayed back and forth, dragging the cart towards one ditch, then the other, that lined either side of the road. Vittorio was seated on the cart, a long switch in his hand that he would strike against the ass, trying to encourage it into a straighter line. When the donkey started to veer right, he'd flick his wrist and a quick snap of the branch to the donkey's right flank followed by a soft bray straightened him. When the tired donkey wanted to go left, a quick backhanded whip righted him once more. Carlo slowed his pace even more, falling back a few steps behind his parents to watch Vittorio awkwardly rolled by. He saw the bags under Vittorio's eyes and the deep lines that had etched their way into his face. His skin had dried and wrinkled like a prune in the harvesting sun. Eyes wide and mouth hanging open, Carlo though that Vittorio looked more and more like a father than a friend.

2. North Africa

Angelo

It was 1942, and the bombs were chasing Angelo a lifetime away from his family. He did not run away from them. He could not run. Dug in on a mucky ridge in North Africa, his regiment had been ordered to hold their ground at all costs. Moisture from the damp earth seeped through his fatigues and permeated his flesh, soaking him through to his bones. His limbs ached. Thankfully standing their ground involved very little movement, which meant struggling against the weight of his drenched clothes and weakened body was unnecessary.

Hunkered down in their trenches, enemy mortar fire couldn't get to them. That didn't stop them from coming as close as they could, however. Each impact sent sprays of sodden earth cascading through the air and down into their hovel. The earth beneath Angelo seemed to vibrate constantly with the assault, and his ears rang incessantly as each rumble of Allied mortar fire was answered with a barrage of Axis gunfire. The scent of dirt and cordite hung heaving in the air. At a stalemate for what felt like days, the only accomplishment of these actions was to deafen the soldiers and line the pockets of munitions manufacturers.

Laying prone against the steep slope of the trench, Angelo's ID tags slipped out of his button-down jacket as the artillery impacts continued to shake the earth. Dangling from the steel ball chain around his neck, the tags were promptly met by a shimmering cross and cornetto. Swinging from their own fine gold necklace, they struggled out of his uniform as well. His mother had given him the cross on the day of his confirmation, and Anna had given him the eland-shaped horn on their wedding day, but it wasn't the memory of those two people that struck a chord with him. It wasn't the tags with his family name stamped on them, a name synonymous with home, that pulled his mind miles away. It was the man who sat in the dirt beside him, shaking and shivering, who made Angelo think of his home, of Cassino.

The man's name was Bruno. That's all Angelo knew about him. That's about all any of them really knew of each other, save for their military aptitudes. He knew that Bruno was a good point man, had a relatively steady shot, and that he'd give his life for the squad. He knew Bruno smoked Alfa cigarettes, but really, who didn't? He also assumed Bruno was a little quirky, since he had a habit of tying his socks together and wearing them like a bandana across his forehead. Aside from those basic facts, he didn't know anything else about the man he now lived beside and could very well die beside.

He didn't know that the lined and wrinkled face, dark as fresh rich soil, came from harvesting fields of olives in the high southern sun. He didn't know that the slight skip in Bruno's step was from an injury he suffered when he nearly fell down a well in the village he grew up in when he was nine. He also didn't know that, despite his complaining, being a soldier in the army was exactly where Bruno wanted to be, for it meant he was free of slaving on his boss's plantation. Most importantly, he didn't know that Bruno could never afford shoes, and that was the reason why he didn't wear his socks. He wanted to know exactly what it felt like to wear something so new and sturdy on his feet.

Angelo squinted up through the hazy veil of smoke as another shower of detritus rained down on them from above. The whistle of the shells sounded as though they were getting closer and closer, and each thudding impact felt like it could have been mere inches away, but he knew that was just his nerves getting the better of him. The shells were falling just as far away as they were an hour ago, and they would be falling at the same distance an hour from now. He wondered how they could maintain the incessant barrage. It was like all the ordinance of the war had been rerouted to this battlefield, both sides taking everything their countries had to offer in an unending contest of one-upmanship.

When he looked down at Bruno again, he didn't see the young man with grease smeared across his face, eyes in a perpetual state of bewilderment. Instead of his scarred, cracked lips full of mud and spittle, Angelo saw the tender pouting lips of his four-year-old Carlo back home. He saw the soft rounded forehead of his two-year-old Antonia under the bruises and welts that marred Bruno's face. He saw the innocent yet mature eyes of his eight-year-old Guido and nine-year-old Paolo instead of the horrified, shell-shocked eyes that were really there, pulsing in Bruno's sockets. Then he saw them all in the ditch. Not Bruno and Angelo and the rest of their troop, but the frail, innocent bodies of his sons and daughter, lying in the ditches of wars twenty, thirty, and forty years hence, as his own father must have foreseen a generation before. And he saw men, other people's children, looking at Paolo, Guido, Carlo, and Antonia, and knowing how well they could shoot or how well they conserved rations. These strangers would know how loyal his children were but would know nothing about their families, about their lives, about who they really were.

Before the sun had baked off the foggy dew of the next morning, Bruno was dead. The shipment of sulfathiazole that they had been waiting for didn't make it through the enemy blockade. Without the antibiotics to help his already compromised system, Bruno had lost his fight with the infection that had grown around the shrapnel cut on his leg. The shells never did come any closer, and one day they stopped entirely. Angelo had seen soldier after soldier, compatriot after compatriot, friend after friend, succumb to the horrors that had befallen them. The platoon was a ghost of its former self, and the Allies marched through them like a scythe through ripe wheat. So few were still alive — and those who were had no strength left to be of any consequence — that the position fell without contest.

3. Kenya

Angelo

When Angelo was taken, through a half-feverish haze, he watched as his captors stepped on Bruno's body. Their dark boots trampled him, mashing his lifeless face into the muck as they ushered what was left of the troop out of the trenches and on to the scorched field above. Within a few weeks, Angelo found himself waking up on soft dark earth behind a wall of barbed wire. His new home in Kenya hadn't even been built when he arrived; it had bene up to him and the other broken men to construct their own prison. Made of a metal roof and wooden walls, their cell was a rectangle twelve feet by twenty and about five paces away from the next, virtually identical structure. The fence surrounding the perimeter was chain link covered in chicken wire and interwoven with barbed wire. He couldn't tell how deep the support poles that held the wire and chain link had been driven, but he knew manpower alone couldn't budge them.

During the day, the earth was hard and unforgiving, only softening overnight when they weren't allowed out of the confinement of their barracks and their slumbering bodies sank inches into the muck. Armed guards stood sentry day and night at the perimeter—they stood in silence mostly, only occasionally berating their captives in a language they couldn't understand. Accommodations aside, Angelo found the air had a hot freshness to it that smelled of humid vegetation, but beneath that familiar odour was still the lingering scent of war. That putrid stench was in Angelo's skin now, permeating his flesh. He felt sure he'd never be able to wash away the stench of all that death.

Angelo's barracks were the first of twenty-four along the road that led to the centre of the base. He and his mish-mashed collection of Germans, Moroccans, and Algerians were the first to see anyone arrive, and they, in turn, were one of the first things the new arrivals saw aside from the three stone archways announcing the camp. Of course, his time spent about the twelve by twenty-foot building was heavily mitigated by the near-constant marching they were led on throughout the camp. For more than six hours a day, they were paraded from one end to the other, around the dusty field, and back to their makeshift home, only to be dragged nearly right back out on the same trek twelve hours later. Understaffed and overworked, it was the most efficient way for the smattering of armed guards to keep everyone in line. It kept prisoners occupied, in order, and, most importantly, tired. The dirt road they trod constantly in front of their abode seemed to stretch nearly as far the eye could see, nothing but dry, dead land spread to the sparse, squat tree line that stretched to the south and east, underscoring the slight incline of a mountain range that broke the flat horizon. To the north lay a smattering of dead trees that mirrored the eight-foot posts that cordoned off incarceration from freedom. Despite his proximity to the other twenty-three buildings, Angelo couldn't tell with any certainty how many other prisoners of war were interned with him, save the other seventy or so in his immediate proximity. Their constant occupation kept them too busy to know or care who else was there; only the incessant moaning, groaning, and crying that permeated the still night air hinted at the sheer volume of interned soldiers. The brief moments of respite were punctuated by an overweight German who, whenever it suited him—which turned out to be most often in the quietest moments—would blurt out something or other in German and shake like a recoiling machine gun.

"Schweineficker! Hurensöhne! Wir werden Sie minderwertig schlachten! Heil dem herrenrasse!"

He'd holler at no one, face ballooning into a red sphere, and then fall to the floor and sob, his bulky form gyrating like a lump of pig fat. Angelo did his best to try and ignore him.

Time dragged on, and the German grew weak. He kept his burly bulk, but his flesh tightened considerably, and the pockets of his mass seemed to hang from his bones like poorly filled sacks of grain from a farmhand's yoke. His thick bones began to press against his flesh, his ribs pressed out from his distended stomach when he'd wheeze in deeply, and yet he still refused to eat most of the proffered foods. It wasn't inedible, the overly bland watery bean-broth that passed for soup, and hard stale bits of bread, but it was just enough to get you out of bed in the morning and move your bowels twice a week. When Angelo awoke one morning to find the German man gone, he bowed his head and said a little prayer. He didn't know him and couldn't understand him, but a life lost was a life lost, and so he wished him peaceful rest in the hereafter.

Making their circuit of the premises once again, on an unremarkable day with the African sun blazing high overhead, Angelo caught a glimpse of something familiar. Something that reminded him of his life outside the wire-and-wood desert camp. Something from back home. He had made his way along with an entourage of other men as close to the fence lining the main road outside their encampment would allow them to await the arrival of a new flock of prisoners. It wasn't much, but as entertainment ran thin, it was something to break the monotony of the daily ritual. As the smudge of shadow in the distance focused, Angelo could see it was another group of Axis soldiers being marched towards their new accommodations.

As the men passed, floating on a cloud of dust, Angelo caught sight of a slightly elongated nose he thought he recognized and a familiar pair of sunken eyes. It was only for a split second, and then the man hobbled past, but Angelo was sure — as sure as he was that it wouldn't rain and the day's ration would be paltry — that it was Giuseppe.

"Giuseppe?" The whisper of his name, foreign after so long, slipped past his lips in a question.

"Giuseppe!" He tried to stammer out with more authority, but his voice caught in his throat as he spoke, really spoke, for the first time in what felt like ages. His feet started shuffling against the beaten sand, kicking up small plumes of dust on this side of the fence as he tried to push through the crowd of detainees. Stumbling into the wall of men, he caught himself and quickly craned his neck to see if he could find his old compare, but the sea of curly black hair pocked with taller blonde crests blurred into one mass of people.

For the next several weeks Angelo tried to get a message halfway across camp. Unfortunately, the armed guards only yelled for him to get away from the fence. Pressing his luck, Angelo called at anyone passing by the barbed wire enclosure. Whether they were German, Italian, or English, whether they were a POW or even a soldier, he would call out to them.

"Prega, di . . . di inviare questo messaggio a . . . a . . . a qualcuno chi chiamo Vittorio."

He said it to anyone who glanced his way, gesturing wildly with all four fingers in an open palm down the roadway towards the other internment camps.

"Io . . . io . . ." He repeated, tapping his chest to signify it was himself he spoke about. "Io, Angelo, sono il suo amico da . . . da . . . da Cassino. Io sono . . ."

Angelo's hands shook slightly with anticipation, every fibre of his being willing a tall skinny man who happened to look his way to understand him. He never thought he'd see anyone he knew ever again, especially not here in Africa. For three weeks Angelo persisted with his crusade, miming his intentions to any who would look his way.

Then his spirit broke. His whole life, it seemed, had been a struggle. Growing up in a world crippled by destruction and loss, his young life had rushed past in a blur. Rushed, that is, until a moment of reckless passion had brought his childhood to an abrupt and ceremonious halt in front of an altar as he was hastily married to a pregnant woman four years his senior. A woman he barely knew. Anna. Then there was the struggle of feeding a growing family on meagre means and the attendant uncertainties of fatherhood. Now Angelo was tired of struggling and abandoned his plight and closed himself off from the others, shuffling through each day with the rest of the cattle in their zombified state, affording barely a grunt of acknowledgement to those around him.

4. Kenya

Angelo

One afternoon, after they had finished their march and were retired to their quarters, one of the guards came by to rouse them. He formed them all in line and shuffled them out the door, an unscheduled march perpendicular to their usual circuit. They were heading clear across camp towards the officers' keep. Eyes wide, Angelo gazed around at the dozen other faces, all from his barracks, most solemn, a few stunned. Stretching his neck to peer over their heads, he saw no other men joining them on this peculiar march.

Shouldering Serafino, another Italian who had been moved to their group not too long after the pudgy German had died, Angelo grunted and jutted his chin towards the direction they were travelling. With the thumb and forefinger of his right hand he made a twisting motion, asking what was going on.

"Loro non vogliono che diventiamo finochio," said Serafino as they walked.

Angleo squinted in confusion. Finochio? What could possibly be in the officers' barracks that would stop them from turning *that* way?

When they got across the field, they were directed towards a small building tucked in behind the officers' building. It was a squat building, made of corrugated tin panels with a roof that sloped towards the back. There was a single door right in the middle of it, flanked by officers on either side. The prisoners were lined up one behind another and ushered in one at a time. One would go in, and about ten minutes later they would come out. As Angelo got closer to the front of the line, he could see the men leaving, each with a cock-eyed bewildered looks on their faces.

Serafino nodded at the guards as he passed by them through the doorway, the guards tilting their heads ever so slightly in acknowledgement. About ten minutes later, Serafino strode out, running his fingers through his slightly matted hair, his damp dark locks shimmering in the late afternoon sun. Angelo turned his attention to the door ahead, the threshold into an unknown world, and stepped forward. His eyes darted slightly between the flanking guards and, mid-stride over the doorstep, the one to his right barked at him.

"Hey, you be gentle now. I know how your kind can get on, and there's lots more guys gotta get through here."

The guard lifted his rifle sideways towards the line of prisoners still more than twenty men deep. Angelo nodded, not understanding a single word, and snapped out a curt thank-you in the only broken English he knew and continued into the dimly lit building.

It was dark inside and smelled like sweat. Sweat and dirt, with a stinging current of vanilla and mint. Such an odd aroma, so out of place. There was something else he couldn't quite place.

Another scent that was familiar, but distant. As his eyes adjusted to the sudden drop in light, Angelo could make out a sparse room with a single small wooden dresser on one side, and a tired looking wardrobe beside it with one door slightly ajar. A single incandescent bulb hung from the low ceiling, casting muted shadows about a room that appeared to swim in the swaying light.

As he scanned the room, his eyes stopped on a single steel-framed cot. Seated near the foot of the cot was a woman with a long, thin, almost malnourished face. She wore a plain cotton off-white robe. She smiled at him and patted at the empty spot on the bed beside her, but broke eye contact as she did, focusing through Angelo and losing herself in a stare that seemed to take her miles away from this place. He followed the gaze of her unfocused eyes as best he could before regaining his composure and shuffling towards the bed. He was two strides from her when she refocused her eyes on his, tracking him like a wary prey follows the path of its predator. Two steps later, he stood before her, eyes fixed as an owl, while his head moved back and forth between her and the empty spot in the bed where a slight double divot compressed the thin mattress—a memento of her last patron. She stared up at him, lips pursed, as Angelo stood there unwavering.

"If that's how you want it, suit yourself then."

She murmured and stood up, slipping the robe from her shoulders with a practiced shrug, and slid her arms over Angelo's broad but weakened shoulders. She pressed her body into his, firm breasts pressing at his chest, hips gently flexing at his upper thigh, cantering back and forth. Her long thin face nestled into the crook of his neck, and thin spindly arms draped over him—arms that could never work a field, Angelo thought, or prepare a hearty meal. As he inhaled then, he found that other scent he hadn't quite been able to place when he entered the room. It was the scent of carnations, just like he wore on his lapel at his wedding.

And the Wars Went on Without Him

5. Kenya

Angelo

On a dry, cool day in 1947, the main gates to the camp were opened and the prisoners were lined up once again to march, but this time they were marching to freedom through the open gates of heaven from the hell they had endured. Angelo stood by the door to the place that had been his home for so long. He took it all in, the worn wood around the handle of the door, the smoky glass that filtered the light of the barracks, and the scent of dust everywhere that seemed to grind its way into their skin and sublimate into their nostrils with every drop of sweat. He had no idea how long his internment at the hands of the Allies had been. It certainly felt like years. It was long enough to forget what his life was like before the war, but not long enough to forget his children. He stood there agog, moments of his incarceration flitting by his periphery like cards shuffled before a flashbulb. He stood there in anticipation of what lay beyond the life that had become so familiar to him in such a short time.

Angelo craned his neck towards the river of POWs as it began to flow into a sea of bobbing heads, all bounding towards freedom. As he scanned the crowd, he could pick out people he had come to recognize from his time there. They all had names he didn't know, and he'd soon forget the nicknames he had given them in his mind. Mostly blonde and brunette coifs bounded by and his eyes glassed over, watching the undulating tide of them pass until he saw a shock of jet-black curls shuffling steadily through the crowd. Angelo's frozen frame snapped into motion and he started to push his way through the crowd towards the black mass somewhere just off centre of the torrent of bodies. He was moving slightly against the surge and, like fighting the waves of Ostia, he kept getting hurtled off of his desired trajectory.

Determination won out, and as a smile cracked his parched lips, Angelo approached the familiar face that supported that dark mane of curls. He stretched his arms as wide as he could in the tightly packed group for an embrace, but as Giuseppe passed by, Angelo froze. His arms suspended empty as the corners of his lips dropped. This man had Giuseppe's face, but his eyes were those of a stranger. The man stared at Angelo in confusion, his eyebrows knitting before being swept up in the current, continuing along with the herd of lost souls passing by. Angelo's arms fell to his sides and he stood motionless, a rock dividing the sea of people as they passed. After a time, he too turned and joined the mass exodus allowing himself to be swept back to freedom and his life in Cassino.

And the Wars Went on Without Him

6. Italy

Angelo

In the assumed familiarity of his home, he found a woman by the name of Carmella raising his three surviving children, Guido, Carlo and Antonia. Anna had died in the bombing of Monte Cassino along with his eldest son, Paolo. His cries during childbirth, a distant echo in Angelo's memories, now conflated with the boy's imagined screams of death.

He married Carmella, this woman who had provided for his family when he could not, this woman with a chubby face and nice round arms that could work a field, prepare a hearty meal, and hold a family together. He married her, even though she was a decade his junior, and he continued his life with her, fathering three more children and moving away from that place of war, that place of death, of lost friends and neighbours.

Angelo found himself on a ship, like the one that deployed him to fight in North Africa, but this time taking him to a whole new world. He lived in barracks of a new kind, with clear windows and a real floor—but still packed full of men. His brethren surrounded him, welcomed him, and helped him. As time soldiered on, so too did Angelo, toiling for his family, fighting to build a life that could contain them all. Soon they came to join him in this new world, one full of such promise and hope, one so new he had to help build it himself from the ground up.

Angelo's children begat children who begat children, and as he felt his march through time coming to a close, his aged body failing him more and more, he thought of the wars he had lived through. Those he had fought and those he had not. Those wars on the battlefield and those in the farmer's field. Those wars of love, of life, of prosperity. He thought of the wars that were now over and hoped new ones would cease with his inevitable departure from the battlefield of life.

But new men took up arms and left loved ones behind.

And the wars began.

Another Bruno with a different name dying for a pointless cause.

And the wars continued.

Angelo sat back watching bombs fall on TV, but he didn't have to run from those bombs, as they were worlds apart and a lifetime away.

And the wars went on without him.

Migrations

1. Toronto, 1966

Angelo squinted as he rolled his shoulder. Pressing the palms of his hands into his lower back, he stretched, arching up from his crouched position bent over a split stake of wood he had just finished driving into the hard, packed earth. Three other men around him were similarly saluting the noon sun as their bodies twisted upward like bindweed. Roberto and Ennio were both Italian, one from the north, one from the south, but they got along just fine. Stas was not Italian. He was Russian. Or Polish. Or something like that—Angelo had never bothered to learn precisely where he was from. Even if he wanted to, he'd probably have difficulty figuring it out. Their badly broken English was all they were able to communicate with, not more than ten words common between them. For the most part, hand gestures sufficed, except when cultural differences got in the way and Angelo's thumbs-up of approval was met with Stas adding copious amounts of water to their cement mixture, resulting in an unusable slop they had to dispose of in the ditch.

Hands still pressed to his back, Angelo turned from side to side, stretching the muscles to either side of his aching spine as he did. Ennio stood by the cement mixer, wiping the beads of sweat from his brow with a thick, hairy forearm. He wore his red-and-white checker patterned button-down shirt over his head like a bandana, the sleeves tied and hanging like tuxedo tails down his back. His thick dark moustache fluttered as he puffed his cheeks and squatted to grab a bag of cement from the ground, hefting it into the open mouth of the mixer. Ennio could make good cement. Stas wasn't bad either, aside from the water incident earlier in the year, but Roberto couldn't mix a decent batch if a chorus of angels sung him the instructions. Angelo himself was a master builder. At least, that was how he saw himself. Back in Italy, his plan was to study under Pier Luigi Nervi in Rome and build structures for all the world to see. Things being as they were at that time in Europe, grand architectural renown had to be left behind, and he found himself here, in a village north of Toronto, pouring curbs along a gravel side street. If it weren't for the multi-storey buildings peeking over the horizon to the south, staring at that dirt road would have made him feel like he was back in Italy, back in those war-poor streets.

—

It was April 1956 when Angelo came bustling into the family home. He had returned from the town square with his purse a little heavier. He had spent most of the afternoon playing cards with other men, gladly relieving them of their sweat-earned money. He had a spring in his step the likes of which Carmella hadn't seen since the feast of the assumption all those years ago. His smile was what attracted her to him. It was broad but not too revealing, his lips curling back in a perfect grin, eyes wide and full of enjoyment. That broad a smile hadn't cracked his face since the birth of their first child six years ago, but Angelo wore it like a badge of delight that day as he swooped through the doorway and into the main area of their home, a kitchen sparsely populated with a table, a bench, and two chairs. He flew to Carmella, carried as if by birds on the tips of his toes, and slid a hand behind her back while his other reached for her open palm.

She hastily ran her hands along her apron, clearing what she could of the flour that coated them. He twirled her around as he murmured a singsong of happiness. She laughed. She couldn't help herself, she just started laughing, so infectious was his joy. Four children came in from the yard at the back of the house. Antonia, Natalia, and Palma with little Benito straddling Antonia's hip as she carried him.

Seeing their parents, they too started smiling and laughing. No one knew why they were so happy—they just were. No one, save Angelo, who had tucked into the front pocket of his trousers a letter from his eldest son, Guido, inviting him to America, where everyone was happy and healthy, without the memories of war all around. To America, where food was so abundant, you just had to sit at any table you saw, and a plate would arrive of the finest meats and vegetables and pastas piled so high they spilled over the sides. No struggling through poor harvests year after year, fearful of where your family's next meal would come from. America, where the streets were not only paved, unlike the snaking, dirt-packed paths of Cassino, but paved with gold.

2. Toronto, 1977

He turned the soil of his meagre plot of land with a bent-edged spade he had salvaged from the bin at work. The handle was perfectly smooth, worn slick with years of toil and sweat. The blade was mildly bent on one end, which was only really an issue if he was trying to carve a straight line through the earth. However, the twisting motion it caused when entering the ground lent itself to turning the soil, making it an amiable weapon in his gardening arsenal.

Sweat ran down Angelo's face, crossing along the lines of his extended forehead, down through the crevasses around his prominent red cheeks, left to pool above his upper lip, swelling his moustache, just starting to pepper with his age. He pulled a handkerchief from the back pocket of his gardener-green trousers and unfolded it with the flick his thick wrist. Dabbing it around his face and down across his chin and neck, he gazed at the late morning sun that hung nearly overhead.

The humidity sank into him, and his gingham shirt hanging unbuttoned halfway to his navel clung to him. Delicately folding the napkin into itself, he scanned his field. A twelve by twenty-foot mound of soil, supported around all sides by monoliths of patio stones hammered vertically into the soil. Angelo's raised garden teemed with dark, rich soil, and sprouts had started from his early spring plantings. Beans, cucumber, and tomato plants all broke the surface of their earthen cradles, reaching for the blessing of life from above while their roots burrowed into the soil in search of the bountiful nutrients hidden below.

Tucking the folded cloth square back into his rear pocket, Angelo took his shovel to the earth again, striking and turning the soil. The lettuce seeds would find good purchase here. He knew they would. And he knew they would provide for his family in a way he could not.

—

It was late summer, 1947, and Angelo had just finished hammering the last dimple of serration into the burgundy-rusted blade of his scythe. The moon was high, bathing the waking fields of wheat in a pale glow that resembled a colourless mid-morning sun. Shadows ran long and severe from the dark tall pines and short fences that dotted his landscape. It was late, but he still had to sharpen the hammered metal blade or there'd be no harvesting tomorrow and, he feared, he was already running late on that. With a creak of joints not nearly as old as they sounded, he pushed himself up from the squat stool. Resting the handle against the side of their home, he stood up straight and arched backwards, hearing his back crackle and his sternum pop. Dragging his tired feet, he shambled to the small wooden shed that hung like a heavy bough of ripe grapes off the side of his house and pulled open a paneled door that whined on its hinges. He rummaged through his paltry collection of tools, spread somewhat haphazardly on the second of three shelves, and pulled out a small round file. Returning to his scythe, he sat and methodically stroked the blade at a tight angle along each hammered depression.

He stared long and hard at the dancing grey stalks of wheat before him as the ribbed edge of his rasp scraped against the metal blade. He stared, and he smiled. With three children relying on him already, and another on the way, he was determined to provide for his growing family. What they couldn't eat, they could sell, and what they couldn't sell, they could eat. He blinked and watched as his imagination skipped through the years and across the field. His children were growing and harvesting with him. The stalks felled and stacked in the back of their small wagon, pulled by their dog Dino. As his children grew in his vision, so too did the cart, pulled at one point by a small donkey, and then oxen, and finally a majestic horse, prouder than any ridden by the cavalry he'd seen.

After the war and his return to Italy, Angelo had convinced Carmella, the woman who would become his second wife, that they could subsist on the land. There was little work in post-war Italy, the impoverished nation clawing itself out of the depths of fascism and attempting to make a complete about-face. His smile continued to beam out over the land, *his* land, as his mind kept racing through the years and generations. This season was their first, and while the selling of their produce had been somewhat lackluster, Angelo chalked it up to the slow recovery everyone was making at the time. He knew the following year would be better, and the one after that better still. The land provided; he need only reap from it what he sowed. And an even greater pride grew within him, and an even stronger will and determination to not just survive, but thrive, and so his hands moved in double-time, his metal file raining miniscule sparks into the cool evening air as Angelo, farmer and father, dreamed long into the night.

3. Toronto, 1988

Angelo stood on the second step of his rickety, wooden three-step stepladder. The cool evenings were giving way to delectably warm days, but there was still a shiver in the air that early spring morning as he stood before the pear tree, the centrepiece of his urban garden. The old limb lay on the uneven patio stones, stained green with droppings from the adjacent grape canopy, bud-less and dying as it slowly dried. It would make fantastic fuel for his pot-bellied stove that coming winter, the dried aromatic nature of the wood wafting from the stove as it cracked and popped. He always kept a kettle on the stove, the water perpetually at a slow roll, humidifying his abode.

The fresh wound on the tree before him bled a small offering of sap as he worked his hooked knife into it, carving down a small wedge an inch and a half deep. The tree stayed steadfast, the remaining branches still clawing at the sky for the sunlight beaming down on them. Angelo hefted a new arm of roughly the same girth proffered from an apple tree whose root system had withered and was slowly choking the life from the limb. The raw end of the apple tree branch had a corresponding wedge carved into it, and he married it to the pear tree. Resting the branch on his shoulder while he worked, he splinted the wounded arm and bound it with tape and twine, tethering it to other limbs as a doctor may bind broken toes to one another to limit movement.

He blinked, and it was 1938, and there was a man screaming as his severed arm lay on the floor before him. The heat of the blast had nearly cauterized the wound, but blood still pumped out of Luigi's split artery in copious amounts. Another soldier in a white helmet emblazoned with a bright red cross knelt beside the one-armed man, working a twisted knot of fabric over the remaining stump and cinching it tightly to stem the flow. The scream faded as sound returned to Angelo—his commander's voice barking orders at him.

They were to take down a tree. A tree? In all this carnage and mess, their priority was a tree? But today Angelo was part of a detachment who wasn't supposed to see front-line battle. It was their job to clear the way for the assault force that would follow and felling trees and digging trenches were all part of that assignment. It was the digging that had rendered Luigi armless, as his shovel struck a landmine.

Angelo moved methodically, carting the Modello 1914 over to the tripod Diego had assembled and dropping into place. The sounds were deafening as the recoil plunged the feet of the machinegun's stand two inches into the earth. The tree before them, an elm with thick branches curved around it like an umbrella, nearly touching the earth, began to splinter and crack. Diego ran the Modello in clockwise concentric circles, slowly eroding the tree from the outside in. The cracks of splintering wood were barely audible over the rapid fire of the fully automatic rifle, and Angelo looked on, stone faced, as the tree, older than he and Diego combined, fell defenselessly to their assault. More trees fell, all about him, as his eyes grew wider, and fires sparked up in the grassy plains, erasing nature from the landscape.

He closed his eyes tight and, opening them, found himself on his ladder. He was in his garden with his freshly grafted tree dripping sap at the new joint. Taking a deep breath, he felt it catch in his throat and fall short of his lungs. His hands shook slightly, fingers tightening into arthritic knots. His left arm ached, then went numb, and as he slowly stumbled back off the ladder, he saw the trees around him sway, their dance of shimmering brilliance moving to the whistling song of the wind, and he wondered—for that brief moment of consciousness he had left— if he would see that same glorious decadence of nature's waltz ever again.

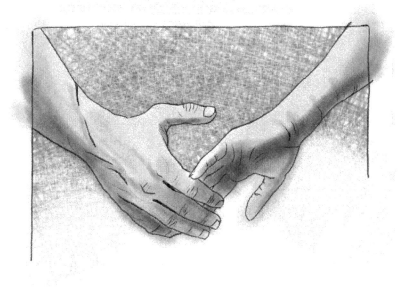

Seven Song

Angelo sat upright on his bed, his lower half disappearing beneath crisp white sheets. The crepe-like fabric crinkled and squeaked when the bed flexed beneath his insignificant weight. The din of the fluorescent ballast buzzed like a wasp. Hushed mumbling came from the hall somewhere as well as the sound of distant snoring sound at the very periphery of his perception. The symphony of ambient sounds was drowned beneath the music that poured forth from somewhere deep within him. His lips never parted, yet an endless stream of whimsical and uplifting songs ran through him. The lyrics of the songs burbled over each other and flowed and ebbed like meandering streams feeding a river with endless switchbacks—one word never quite finishing before the next began, an endless loop of ever-present vocalization. As the light of the tube overhead spilled its sickly hue just beyond the edge of the bed and began to diffuse across the speckled linoleum floor, figures were visible encircling him where he lay. Mottled caricatures of men and women, they sat in astonishment, joy, contemplation, and sorrow as the music continued to flow in foreign tongues and disparate melodies from his core.

One of the faces from the amorphous ensemble came into focus, almost leaning in as a teller of tales might to draw their audience further into their fable. He beat his half-formed fist against his head twice as the firelight flicker of illumination revealed the stranger to be Guido. Only it wasn't Guido, not the aged Guido, whose life had been cut short as his mortal flesh succumbed to the ravages of brain cancer—unable to process simple functions towards the end, his deterioration became a mockery of a once proud life. No, it wasn't *that* Guido, but a youthful Guido full of life and full of joy. A vibrant Guido who used to share a gallon of homemade wine with his stepfather, the bitter spirit stinging from the moment it hit their lips until the moment it struck their bellies. The Guido who played guitar best after everyone had had their fill of that homemade wine. The Guido whose smile cracked his face ear-to-ear and brought joy to life's best and worst moments. The Guido Angelo had forgotten.

The music carried on while the assembled spectres began to disperse. The melodies had begun to fight with the growing rumble to his right as furnaces struck their flame and spewed forth their heat into the cold winter night. Anna came up to him too, from somewhere beyond his vision and outside of his reality. Her face was immaculate, an identical porcelain cast of his fondest memories of her. Gently lined with the experiences of life and love and as bone-pale and supple as it was in 1938 when he last saw her. When he last pressed his lips to hers at the docks in Naples as he scampered aboard the ship that would whisk him away to another life. How could he have known that was the last he would see of her? Her perfect imperfections, those things that make an individual *individual* had been erased from her like a re-touched photograph Angelo never knew his mind had. Behind his first wife stood Carmella, her visage unaltered by the cleansing filter of memory. Lines and blemishes and imperfections abounded, her presence almost real, almost tangible. Signaling her presence to Anna with his eyes, his silence pleaded with her for direction.

"You go with her, Angelo."

Her voice, nearly angelic, caressed Angelo's aged ears and soothed his aching memories. Perfectly serene and at peace, bathed in a softly shimmering pool of pure white light.

"She is a good woman."

Her mouth didn't move, lips never parting, tongue never curling to form the words she spoke. Her words came from deeper within, they came from her heart, from her soul. They came from a place deeper than language could represent. The words were simply feelings, emotions given form and function.

"You stay with her . . ."

Anna spoke again from beyond the limitation of speech, and her hand floated towards him open-palmed. Angelo's eyes flashed open against the under-lit ceiling of the hospital. The lunch cart with one intermittently squeaking wheel moving outside in the hall echoed throughout the ward. The tight-piled carpeting that used to trap even the faintest odours had been ripped up ages ago and been replaced by the unforgiving nature of linoleum.

"Carmel . . ." he called out, his grey-green eyes transfixed on nothing on the ceiling, focusing beyond it to the heavens beyond.

His wife jumped from her chair by his side, a slight groan of vinyl reshaping itself. She leaned her body in towards him, her left hand falling to his, holding it tenderly as a child might caress a kitten. He blinked. Twice. Shaking his arthritic hands towards his face from a small box of tissues on the table adjacent to his bed he began dabbing the corners of his eyes.

"Carmel," he said, "I hear music."

His eyes widened when he said *music*, pushing years of experience aside in the wrinkles that had piled on the outside edges of his face.

"It's in my head," –the tips of his fingers tapped rapidly against his temple– "but I can hear the most beautiful music you could ever imagine."

The songs were sung in seven distinct languages, all at once separate and simultaneous. Seven languages, none of which Angelo understood, and yet they all made perfect sense to him. A slight smile broke Carmella's stone-serious face—the deep-set lines wrinkling around the corners of her mouth in small accentuating tracks. Her husband never spoke like this. He never took the time to reflect on the beauty of things, and especially never took the time to expound on it to her.

"And I see Guido, Carmel."

The lines in her face fell back to their natural resting places, running down her cheeks like shallow-tilled soil. Her lips puckered as she tried to choke back sad memories. Her tears would have betrayed her stalwart stance had Angelo glanced over, but his eyes hadn't left their vigil on the mesmerizing nothingness before him. "And Paolo is here, and Anna . . . my . . . my first wife . . . and Maria . . . Maria my sister . . . you don't know them . . . they died before I met you . . ."

His eyes continued to widen, enthralled yet unfocused.

The wrinkled fat of Carmella's belly and arms jiggled slightly as another tear swelled her eyes. She dared not blink for fear of her falling tears pulling Angelo from his joyous revelry beyond the veil. Her rational mind worked hard to convince herself that Angelo was merely at the mercy of the cocktail of drugs coursing through his veins. He wasn't really seeing and hearing things; it was just his mind playing tricks on him. Just like her mind was making her believe her husband wasn't experiencing these visions. Her daughter had told her that Demerol would cause hallucinations. She told her these drugs would pull things from Angelo's mind that even he wasn't aware were there and bring them out into a reality more vivid than life itself. She never thought they would be this real to him though, this close.

Carmella's eyes began to dry as she held them open for fear of striking her tears free, but the tears came anyways. Angelo began to talk of Guido again, his lips quivering as he did, mocking his speech like an out-of-sync television show. Carmella had to turn her face quickly as she could hold back no longer and shut her eyes tight, the tears soaking her lashes and staining her cheeks. She tried to muffle the heaving sounds of her sobs with her dried coarse hands as her mind raced and she spiraled down into the well of emotions she had worked so hard to keep herself out of.

He can see them, she thought. *He's that close.*

She sputtered slightly, the two thoughts bouncing about in her skull relentlessly. Her breath caught in her throat before she could let out a bleat of sorrow, and she thanked the saints for the strength to hold on just a little longer.

"Carmel . . ." Angelo called, banishing her thoughts temporarily.

His head turned slightly towards her, but his unwavering gaze remained transfixed on the visions he saw beyond the ceiling above. Swallowing deeply, Carmella turned back to Angelo. She ran her stubby fingers along the dark, purple channels under her eye sockets to wipe away her tears. She leaned in closer to her husband and laid her small thick hands on his long skinny ones once again.

"Where is Carlo?" he said. "He always loved me so much. That poor fool."

Carmella choked back another sob, the thick knot of it holding painfully in her throat. Angelo blinked. Then again. His eyes opened each time to their fullest. He then turned towards Carmella and let his gaze fall upon her completely. He stared at her for a long moment, his breathing quick and shallow, his eyes large and vacuous, his heart emotionless. Then his lip began to quiver. His thin cracked bottom lip shook almost imperceptibly. The crow's feet about his face puckered as his eyes began to gloss. He finally blinked, and when he did his right hand moved swiftly in shutter-stop motions to bring a napkin to his face to hide his tears.

"I just want to see him again," he said, his voice cracking slightly. "I need to see him. I know, soon as he walks through that door, I can go."

The tears flowed freely now, rolling through the deep crevasses in Angelo's face. The tissue did nothing as the gathered tears fell in gentle droplets to his pajamas, darkening the fabric. Carmella gripped her husband's hand tighter and let her tears fall too as they sat there sharing their final moments in silence.

But beyond the waking world the songs continued singing. All the words of the seven songs spilling upon one another, yet each heard as crisp and clear as a new dawn. All seven songs sang softly in seven foreign tongues for Angelo long into his last night.

Sins of Man

1. Rome, 1944

Nicola called orders as he plowed through the trench, his coal-black leather boots sinking three inches into the mucky mess that pooled at the bottom of the man-made swale. Tiny drops of mud splattered across the shiny patent leather, marring their perfect patina. Squishing into another step, he continued his tirade of commands. His instructions came instinctually, a part of his brain operating outside of conscious thought with a will unto itself. The words he barked, ingrained into his psyche through months of training, an automatic response to the pounding echoes of mortar fire. His conscious mind, on the other hand, existed behind that trained mind, ignorant of the war that raged all about him. That part of his mind, the still human part, was thinking about his wife and children, crammed in a cave under the pillars of smoke and fire that had once been Monte Cassino. He could imagine the whistle of each bomb through the air above their tiny heads, the explosive impacts melding into a constant, reverberating drone that shook the earth and his family to their cores. All the children being tossed about by the suddenly shuddering world, bouncing uncontrollably between jagged rocks and crying mothers.

These spectres haunted the periphery of his vision as he continued his militant tirade, squishing through the mud and turning over body after body of dead or dying children. Children under his command, children in his charge. Each youth bearing the face of his own sons Rocco and Stefano. The images of his daughters Sophia and Natalia danced about his mind. His wife Maria was only a voice, echoing in his skull, warning him to be careful as they parted ways that fateful night in 1942.

Nicola came to a soldier, face down in the dirt, his blonde curly hair cascading down the back of his neck towards his bare, badly scared back. Deep, uneven lacerations across his shoulder blades brought the voices and images battling in Nicola's mind to a cacophonous crescendo. He turned over the strange mess of a man who lay motionless at his feet, and all at once the symphony in him came crashing down into a void of silence. As the soldier's eyes fluttered open, Nicola froze, his mind and body locked in the deep radiant blue of this man's gaze. In those azure pools, Nicola saw his wife again, and as the soldier parted his parched lips ever so slightly, he heard her name Maria.

"Marya . . ." The whisper, barely audible, seemed to come *through* this pale, naked man and not *from* him. He raised his hands in weak supplication and defence, dirt ground into his otherwise pristine palms. His taut, almost porcelain-white flesh was pulled over clearly visible ribs that barely moved as he breathed, steady and deep. Other than the streaks of dirt and those two horrid wounds on his back, the man's flesh was flawless.

A half-dozen rifles were instantly trained on the strange man as a barrage of wooden stocks smacked against shoulders in a crisp echo of military paraphernalia. Nicola's men glared down the oiled barrels of their bolt-action carcanos at the stunned man.

"Nemico o Alleato?" snapped Ernesto, the man to Nicola's right, in sharp Italian.

Barely a boy really, Nicola expected Ernesto's voice to crack every time he spoke. His rifle remained slung over his shoulder by its thin leather strap. Splayed across his palms lay a small book, no bigger than a Sunday missal, with a frayed ribbon marker dangling from the top, open two-thirds of the way through. His grimy finger traced across the page, following his scrawled notes as he read in stilted English.

"Enemy or ally?"

Flashing his shimmering young eyes at the stranger with a brief pause, he returned to the pocketbook and continued reading from its yellowed pages tracing a stuttering finger along each line as he did.

"Feindlich oder Verbündeter?"

"Inimigo ou Aliado?"

He continued through the list of languages, scrawled phonetically, struggling as the words found purchase on his tongue.

"Ennemi ou Allié?"

"¿Enemigo o Aliado?"

The stranger's eyes, wide as cue balls, darted around. He focused on no one, like a cornered mouse, twitching his senses in every direction for an escape route. His deep pink lips, full and supple under the splatter of mud that adorned half his face, parted and he barbled out something incoherent.

"ܐܝܠ ܘ ܪܐܝܢܝ

The men exchanged wary glances. Nicola's eyes narrowed, his squint dissecting the man for a moment. Then, with a cinematic flourish of his right hand in the air, he announced his conclusion.

"Tedesco."

And why not? He certainly *could* be German. If he wasn't, they'd just have to sort that out later.

Two of his men released their rifles to hang impotently from their straps and threw a sheet over the man's shoulders as Ernesto pocketed his small book and bound the stranger's hands. Nicola, squinting once more, rocked up onto the balls of his feet to feign a glare across the waking plain. He could see no way for this lone German—if indeed that's what he was—to have navigated no man's land, naked, without incident. Of course, there were those gashes on his back. On his knees beside Nicola, the man heaved in deep breaths.

The very air around them seemed to quake as they dragged this walking corpse through the beaten landscape. He tripped and stumbled on bare feet, as if his body were only now discovering his extremities, learning how to walk for the first time. The shack they brought him to seemed to be made of mud, for whatever used to constitute the walls was now caked with it. The high-pitched whistles became muffled hums once inside the building, their volume and timbre only returning when nearby impacts would rattle gaps into the structure, allowing the free flow of sound through their parted openings.

"We found him in the northern ditches," one soldier said.

His voice bounced quickly between the floor and the tin roof, running off down the corrugated channels just slowly enough for the echo to rattle across their ears. They stood in a makeshift office, complete with a tank-green shoulder-height filing cabinet and a large wooden desk. There was a map strung up against one wall showing what appeared to be hundreds of concentric circles each equidistantly spaced across the surface with smaller target-like circles occasionally breaking their smooth curving paths. There was a standard bearing a tired looking Italian flag behind the desk, which itself was adorned with a smattering of scattered papers, all held down by a random assortment of reconstituted munitions enjoying a second life as paperweights. There was even a coat rack with a bowler cap and thick grey woolen coat hanging from it in the corner.

The gruff, aged man behind the desk chewed at his Toscano as he stared at the sight before him. Alfonso had seen a lot of things before the war, and even more since it had started, but he had never seen anything like this. Three men, two of them his soldiers, one a stark-naked blonde man covered in filth and draped in a military issue emergency blanket. Both Italian soldiers stood at attention, one of them holding the sheeted man upright, his arm interwoven with the pale stranger.

Alfonso stood from his seat, wood creaking as he relieved it of his weight,

"You found him like *this*?" He motioned out an open palm at the scene splayed out before him, punctuating the bizarre condition the stranger was in.

Though the journey from the northern trenches had dragged the stranger through more mud, and though raining dirt had stippled his exposed flesh and nestled into his hair, the odd cleanliness and obvious nakedness of his pale body remained intact.

"We believe he's German."

The first soldier spoke again as if following a preprogrammed dialogue, answering Alfonso's unasked question.

Releasing a heavy sigh, Alfonso took the cigar from his mouth with an elaborate gesture that involved the entirety of his arm swinging about, motioning for the two soldiers to seat the man.

Alfonso remained standing, shifting his weight upon his hips, his eyebrows alternating likewise, in a dance of curiosity.

"Fetch the interpreter," he barked, and before he could finish the order one of the soldiers had already taken off in a brisk trot, his kit jingling slightly.

Alfonso rested his hands on his hips momentarily and drew a mouthful of smoke.

"We'll get to the bottom of this soon enough, crucco."

Grabbing the Toscano from his gaping maw, he crossed his arms and chewed over the warm smoke in his mouth. A lazy trail of white drifted up from the tip of the cigar as its pungent stench began to fill the cabin making the cramped space feel smaller and smaller. Placing the cigar in the brown glass ashtray that seemed to grow out of the top of the desk, he nestled his grey-stubbled chin into the palm of his left hand as his right hand held his left elbow. He tapped his index finger against his thick cracked lips. The momentary silence was broken by a thud outside that rattled the seams in the walls once more allowing the piercing whistles to stab their way into the stranger's brain.

"Good day."

The interpreter called as he entered the ramshackle building. He shook his head, poking at his ears with a twisting index finger as if trying to unclog the hollow sound of nothingness stopping up his hearing. Alfonso returned to his seat behind the desk, slinking back as a snake would recoil to its nest. The interpreter pulled a small steel chair from the wall and positioned it across the desk at a safe distance from the stranger. He straddled the chair's wood slat seat and crossed his legs tightly at the knee. Opening a large leather-bound notebook across his peaked thighs, he pulled a pen from the stitched loop within. Touching it to his tongue, he paused. The room fell silent and the sounds of war melted in the distance. The stranger had taken the silence of the room as an invitation to speak.

ܪܝܐܝܪܝ ܐ.ܐܪܝ ܪܝܐܪܐܠܐܐ ܩܠܐ—ܐܝܪܝ ܡܐ ܐܪ"

"Ask him his name," said Alfonso as if the stranger hadn't spoken.

"Wie heissen Sie?" the interpreter said, his gaze focused on the stranger, penetrating him as his pen poised to strike the page beneath.

"Wie . . . Sie?" Repeated the stranger in a stammer. Confusion settled in his voice and his eyes flitted between the two men. Panic rose in him briefly before his shoulders slumped slightly and his strength slipped from his spine.

And so it went: dictated command in Italian followed by mechanically translated German, and finally a choppy parroted response from the stranger. The stranger worked hard to form the odd German words around his broken unknown tongue. It felt ages ago the soldiers had brought him in, proclaiming he was German, and indeed, in time, the language he spoke did *become* German.

2. New York, 1985

He pulled her head back as she screamed, fingers twisted into the long wavy brown locks that draped down her sweat-slick back. Arched in a sharp curve, eyes wide, chin jutting and mouth agape, she froze in the moment of pulsating passion before her body slumped down against his. The slick flesh of their heaving chests pressed against each other, lungs swelling in an out of synch pattern that complemented each other as only lovers' inconsistencies can. Her head lifted mid-breath, damp hair framing her angular face as it pooled about his slowly-blinking eyes. Sweat quickly cooled against her smooth breasts and his lightly haired chest. He fluttered his eyes quickly, blinking away her dark strands as her pouting lips cracked a smile and her body bucked slightly in a silent giggle. She slid off him, the thin sheets sticking to her cheeks making it a stilted, jagged motion. He sighed deeply as he fell out of her, eyes refocusing on the stippled ceiling above him as his chest rose and fell.

She got out of bed and took a step towards the door

"Maya," he called, more a statement than question.

She paused without turning around, her naked form in mid-stride.

"Yes, Martin?"

But he did not answer. His eyes remained transfixed on the ceiling, his breath slowing to short sharp gasps. He blinked. Twice. Then turned slowly to his side, back to her, and tucked his hands up under his pale cheek. He closed his eyes against the cool blue-grey shafts of moonlight permeating the porous sheet of cotton that made up the off-white curtain. The venetian blinds left twisted half-open behind the drab sheets cut the rays into sharp bars, and his mind tumbled back into a prison cell of sleep.

Freefall. Martin's eyes were tearing up, streams running back from the corners, across his temples and pooling in the ruts of his ears. His teeth gritted and lips drew back, the wind cutting deep caverns inside his mouth. The heavy air stung his eyes, the chemicals and pollutants biting at his flesh.

His vision fogged at brief intervals, and he couldn't tell if it was clouds or smoke from the fires of war that he plummeted through. Whatever their cause, the brief moments of reprieve they offered were lost islands in the hellscape of violence all around him. Blinking his blurred vision away, the shocking sight of the bastardized field below assaulted him. Woven with a latticework of ditches and spotted with craters, the field of destruction stretched from horizon to horizon, the beauty of the work of God decimated under the thumb of man and awash in what looked like motes of dark soot and ash.

As he fell, however, the motes became ants, and the ants, men—men unwittingly marching toward their own death among a scarred landscape that had already closed around them like a tomb.

He opened his mouth to pray, but a burning wind tore down his throat and pulled his voice from him. His hands flew to his face, pointlessly shielding him from the earth as the soil struck, compressing the tissue on either side of his hands together, shattering the bone between. The fleshy sheets of fat and tendon offered no cushioning as his nose liquefied, shards of bone from his hands piercing the flesh of his cheeks and forehead an instance before the impact shattered the sharp chiselled lines of his face. His eyes were slashed into gelatinous chunks as the protective curve of his orbital bones compressed in on them. The mass of his bulk continued forcing him downward into the ground, his sinews systematically snapped, organs imploding and collapsing, pierced and compressed by each other part of his form. His hearing remained until the back of his skull completed its trajectory, rending itself from his flesh and destroying his mind. His hearing remained just long enough to hear his soul scream.

Maya turned gently in their bed, her eyes fluttering open as she did. Martin wasn't there. She saw the soft glow of incandescent light beyond the door to their bedroom as she focused out of her sleepy haze. She knew he must have had another nightmare. The same nightmare he kept having. The nightmare of his earliest memory. The memory of a birth and death, simultaneous life and longing.

She rolled to her left, staring absently at the slight impression his body left in the weakened springs of the cheap mattress and the pucker in the pillow where his head had lain. She ran her hand down the cool, bare crevice, imagining each undulation of his taught frame until it sunk beneath the sheets. She may have slid her hand back up, but that may have only been a desire her imagination fulfilled as her breathing became long and deep while her mind tumbled away.

3. Toronto, 1996

Nicola's eyes shot open. The piercing azure pools of that strange blonde man's fractured gaze permeated beyond the veil of his sleep and continued to haunt him in the waking world.

On her regular round, the nurse noticed him stir and shuffled quickly towards him, her soft rubber soles padding gently along the speckled epoxy flooring.

"Now, Nicola," she said in a patronizing whisper as her dark eyes dart back and forth, leaning in towards him as if their conversation were private. "Are you having trouble sleeping? Let's see if we can't get you some codeine."

She began her animated shuffle again as she moved away from him, her pink and white sneakers squeaking once eerily in the silent halls of Mount Sinai. Nicola tried to signal for her to stop and return, wriggling like an upturned beetle against the tight-fitting sheets, stiff as kraft paper.

"No . . . no . . ."

He tried, but his voice was lost to him. His head sank back into the dead-flat pillow, and he sighed, his weakened chest sinking before spasming back out over his hacking breath, the sickly layer of phlegm perpetually coating the walls of his tar-stained lungs fighting against his body's will to survive. His hands shook slightly, swollen arthritic joints locking his fingers in crablike pincers as he looked around in an acute arc. Anxious and nervous, his eyes traced the tether of his emaciated arm to the two plastic bags that hung half-empty above his head. The nicotine curtained cages of the other men in his ward were spread out before him, their dim ochre night lights leaking above and below and bathing the white-grey floor and ceiling in a sickly amber. The scent of age and disinfectant hung in the air like a persistent fog.

Before he could finish taking in the room, the well-meaning nurse shuffled back in, her sneakers making soft sucking noises this time with each of her mouse-like steps.

"Okay hon, I've got . . ."

She said, staring at the small paper cup of narcotics in her hand, only to look up and see his head snuggled against his pillow, heavily creased eyes gently closed, fluttering slightly.

After a moment of peaceful contemplation, her eyes instinctively shot to the screens monitoring his biometrics and, without actually reading the steadily undulating lines and pulsing numbers, assured herself of his comfort. Reaching out she tried to pry his left hand from its tight grip around the safety bars at the sides of his bed, but his thick, yellowed nails were pressed into the ragged flesh of his palm, unrelenting. With each of her gentle tugs, his grip tightened around the cool metal tube. With her hand still covering his, she curled out her lower lip and her head lolled around, her eyes scanning up and down the empty stall for another solution.

Leaving his hand, she saw his tendons relax below his mottled flesh. Taking the upper edge of the mint-green sheet, she tugged up on it, causing it to pull taught over his frail body as it twisted slightly from the opposite side of the bed. With a gentle huff, she convinced herself it would suffice and, after taking one final look at Nicola's resting form, his rib-wide chest swelling and falling beneath his blue hospital robes, she left the room.

4. London, 1962

The button-studded burgundy leather of his high-backed chair wrenched slightly as his shoulder blades flexed with the deep breathing of his swelling lungs stretching his sternum. Straining to maintain the sucking in of his mid-life paunch, he rolled his shoulders upward and back into the chair. The subtly grained oak bookcase ran behind his chair, each volume of text lined up perfectly perpendicular to the shelving. Every spine creased and faded with the gilding worn from their engraved names, their various colours doing nothing to prevent them from blending into one another.

He was accustomed to the noises made by his claw-foot chair, they were the same noises made by the other oxblood chair where Mr. Engels sat, talking. A polished brass nameplate rested atop his wide oak desk: RONALD D. LAING, a name found on the diplomas that hung on the wall behind the desk, and etched in a serif font on the frosted window of the oak door that lay between him and his secretary, Jana, and again on the full-length glass door that opened to the stale gray hallway of the low-rise tower that housed his office.

". . . don't you think that's odd?" said Engels.

"Would *you* say it's odd?"

Dr. Laing's eyes pierced him from a slightly cocked-forward head. The flesh of his sockets oddly bulbous as they overflowed the thickness of his cupped gold reading glasses. Martin Engels glanced down at his thumbs as they pressed into each other over interwoven fingers, the tips pink beneath close-cropped nails.

"I don't know . . . I mean, is it normal to dream about that sort of stuff?"

"Do you consider yourself abnormal?"

"Well . . ." His eyes darted up from the whitening tips of his thumbs.

His vision floated, trying to focus beyond the doctor's head at the arrangement of volumes stacked against the wall. Eventually darting back to his thumbs through a blink, the ridges of his thumbprints resting microns apart.

"I wouldn't say any more abnormal than most people, I guess."

His eyes rose in subservience to Dr. Laing again, but shot to the gaping window to the right of the desk before they could meet the doctors. Daleham Gardens was bustling, or as bustling as could be expected for Daleham Gardens at mid-afternoon. His eyes retraced their progress back to the doctor's judging gaze, then back to his unwavering thumbs and crossed fingers.

Doctor Laing leaned back in his chair. "And you believe others to be abnormal?"

"No, I was just trying to make a little joke. I—"

"So you think these sessions are a joke?" Dr. Laing said, never so much as cracking a smile or raising an eyebrow; he was all business.

Martin scratched at the front of his short blonde hair and grimaced slightly, then ran his fingers through it twice, front to back.

"Look, I don't really care about other people right now. I just want to know why I'm having these horrible dreams. I want to know why I keep dreaming of a life in New York with this Maya woman over twenty years from now. It's feels so real, so matter-of-fact, and yet I am the same age as I am now. What does that mean? And why am I dreaming about the war, about being lost on a battlefield? I'm not even old enough to have been a soldier, and even if I were, why is there no record of my service. Hell, why is there no record of *me*. Actually, doctor," –Martin squirmed, rising slightly– "I don't even really care *why*, I just want to know how to make it stop!"

Ronald Laing sat there for a moment, the butt of his pen resting gently against his lower lip, puckering it ever so slightly. In a smooth languid motion, he moved to start marking his page and, peaking his eyebrows for the first time, spoke after a short shallow sigh.

"So you do not care, as you put it, about others?"

Martin let out a long sigh, then drew a deep breath in through his nose and blew it out through pursed lips. He leaned hard into the back his chair, without the leather-creaking comfort of the doctor's commanding throne.

5. Somewhere in Europe, 1944

He would have been enough of a prison unto himself, lost as he was in a world he did not know, and that did not know him. Trapped in his own mind and surrounded by languages he didn't understand and people he didn't recognize, he was a shallow island in a tumultuous sea. But the allies needed to see him restrained and contained. They needed to imprison him on their own terms, in their own ways. Hours, days, maybe weeks passed as he would wake in darkness, and pass out from exhaustion in the same darkness, always with the smack of blood on his lips. Always with the stench of vomit in his nostrils. Always with the ache of torture in his soul.

They kept him locked up from the day he was found until the day the war ended, in total no more than a year, in an eight-foot stone cube, with one windowless metal door and the constant drip of an unseen leak echoing the seconds of his incarceration. He was visited intermittently by people of import, for any assistance he could offer, by choice or force, in fighting the German machine. They visited in pairs or more, usually in silence. He was interrogated, often naked. And beaten, always naked. He had been tried and convicted by every soldier who visited him without so much as a moment of deliberation. Each guard's whipping belt a judge's gavel, each man's thrusting fist the echo of it in the hollow courtroom.

His crime was quite simple: He was German. At least, he was *told* he was German on that first fateful night in the dark hollow of the trenches. He knew nothing of his life before the moment he was in that ditch in Italy. With no memory, with no history, his mind and body instinctively held onto each moment of his horrid experience building a life for him. Fearing to lose this new life too, his torture defined his psyche, and he became the pain.

Sins of Man

6. Toronto, 1996

The wheelchair. How humiliating. Nicola tried telling his daughter that he once walked six miles on a sprained ankle, carrying a half-dead soldier over his shoulders through mucky, uneven terrain, but without his dentures his words were mumbled, his toothless maw spewing forth virtually unintelligible drivel. Then again, he couldn't really complain. After all, he was going home. Wrapped in an oversized jacket, his legs lashed together in a buffalo check flannel blanket, he sat in silent reflection.

They wheeled the chair out into the cool bite of late Canadian winter where mild mornings could plummet to arctic afternoons. His puffy eyelids spasmed at the gust of chilly wind that swirled up in the entranceway. Instantly tearing up, he blinked away tears as he pulled at the fur lining of the collar of his suede jacket. Trying to stretch it over his exposed neck, he tugged at it to no avail, unable to convince the dead animal to move from beneath his bony seated frame. The forest-green Aerostar was dithered gray with a salt and slush sediment, the lower half of it disappearing into the pale gray of winter-worn asphalt.

Natalie struggled with the chair's brakes, trying to snap them into place before helping her father get out of the chair. Babbling the entire time in an endless stream of drivel, Nicola had no idea what his daughter was saying and strained to push himself off the chair before the locks were fully engaged, making Natalie's work all the more difficult.

He was out of breath by the time he managed to wrestle himself to his feet, determination getting the better of him. He'd be damned if he was going to let his daughter treat him like an invalid, like a child. He was a man, a survivor, a veteran for God's sake! A veteran of life, and of war. Natalie tried to hide her frustration at his pigheaded stubbornness but failed at it miserably. Well, he was frustrated too, he asserted to himself with a grunt.

"Hello, Nonno, how are you?"

His grandson Joseph's voice was barely audible to the old man's aged eardrums. Artillery stricken and machinery worn, he could barely hear anything below a loud call. He tried clambering into the van slower than he lunged out of the wheelchair but realized his mistake the moment Natalie's hand braced against his back. Nicola rolled his eyes and began puffing his sunken cheeks slightly as his daughter pushed against him, helping him into the passenger seat. Small plumes of white billowed from his old grey lips as he huffed. Once seated, and the door closed—a little too forcefully—by Natalie, Joseph tried again.

"Hello, Nonno. How are you?"

This time his basic Italian was a little more defined, a little easier to understand, and a lot louder. After a long-drawn-out sigh, Nicola's response was a simple turning over of his left hand. Rotating it from back to palm then to back again, signifying 'so-so' with an added grunt for emphasis.

The orange-and-mauve brick house ran low to the ground, squashed among the towering beiges and whites of newer homes that had sporadically grown about Nicola's home over the decades he had lived there. Looking around as the van pulled in, Nicola saw the stark contrasts of buildings in a jarring frame-skip of vision as the poorly manufactured sport suspension of the van bounded over the lip of the driveway. It was early March, and still his daughter stopped him when his stiff fingers reached clumsily for the small plastichrome door handle.

"Wait . . . wait Dad . . . wait until we've opened the door to the house . . ."

Her Italian was choppy, a bastardized Canadianization of the broken Italian dialect she grew up speaking. Nicola's eyes rose from his futile attempts at the handle and fell outside the window to one of the tall beige homes. The one they built last year. The Chinese. That's what he called the family that lived there. They were actually a Korean couple with three children who shared their home with their children's grandmother, but they were *the Chinese* to him. Like the other nationalities that surrounded him, he meant no harm in the naming conventions he employed, only simplifying matters for himself. He assumed they called him the Italian. And deep down inside, he believed they all knew what each other was capable of based solely on outward appearances.

By the time he was done thinking about these neighbours he knew only in passing—acquaintances on his journey through the last chapter of his life—he'd climbed the three steps to his porch and was being ushered over the threshold like a tightrope walker being guided out on their first step off the safety of the platform. Shuffling along on his old spindly stilts that cramped and seized with the tidal pulls of the moon, Nicola rushed as best he could for the familiarity of his couch. The twang of the screen door snapping shut behind him announced his entourage filling the room. This new couch was stiffer than the old one he had used for the better part of a decade. This one was green, his last one was brown. The colours meant nothing to him, the symbolism of the earth-tones meant nothing to the farmer-turned-soldier-turned-mason-turned-burden. They were simply the couches that were on sale.

"Dad . . . Dad! Listen to me!"

His daughter nearly had to shout as she leaned into him to pierce the silent echo that hollowed his hearing. Despite years of pleading, he refused to wear a hearing aid. The sounds of the world, silent for so long, assaulted his senses and made his life unbearable.

"You're not allowed to lie down anymore," she said. "Remember what the doctor said? You have to sit up, in this chair!"

She didn't point but twisted her entire torso towards the upright blue vinyl chair that sat adjacent to the doorway to his bedroom, signaling with both arms as an airplane marshaller might guide an aging 737.

"If you don't, the fluid will collect in your lungs again, and we'll be heading back down to the hospital." She paused, measuring her next words carefully. "If you go back again, you probably won't come out, and me and Charlie can't keep waking up at two in the morning to help you . . . We have work to take care of, and Joseph . . ."

Her face wanted to say more, as did the way her intonation trailed in her throat, but she stopped herself.

Sitting briefly on the sofa, hands half-supporting his hunched frame on bruised knuckles, he chewed on his thoughts with his gummy jaw.

"I'll sit where I want to sit," he said in a sharp, gruff tone. "I've sat where I've wanted to for almost ninety years already. I'm not going to change where I sit for you or any doctor. To hell with him, the mother that bore him, the midwife that delivered him, and the saint that cursed him."

His body remained quite motionless, poised as it was on his feeble knuckle support, but his head bobbed about wildly on the fine tendons of his stretched neck, prodding, poking, and swaying, chin jabbing to punctuate his point.

Popping his elbows, he let his body gently fall across the couch. Laying down, he tucked his feet up at one end while he nudged his head into the coarse towel that lay draped over the thinly padded armrest and closed his eyes. He felt so very tired. All he wanted to do was sleep. Why did Natalie always make him get so angry with her? All he wanted to do was sleep. Didn't she know he was tired of it all? He just needed to sleep—just one long, deep sleep.

7. New York, 1985

"Was it the usual one?" Maya asked, her back to Martin as she cracked two eggs into a bowl.

Her body moved mechanically as she dropped the shells on the cool beige Formica counter and picked up the whisk. She beat the eggs into a creamy smooth mass and reached for the small glass saltshaker resting on the back of the yellow stove. Martin skimmed some bubbly froth from the top of his fresh-poured orange juice, softening the dry crusty toast in his mouth before trying to respond.

"Yeah . . . same thing."

His thick tongue working around half the bread that refused to make it down with his first swallow. He blinked slowly, allowing his eyes to unfocus and chewed at the husk in his mouth with distant indifference. He knew the next words that would come out of her mouth. He had heard them oh so many times before. She meant well. Deep down he knew that she did actually believe her futile attempts at helping him would one day bear fruit. But he was tired of hearing her try to help, so he tuned her out, concentrating instead on the grinding sound that came from the left side of his jaw every time he ground his molars into the stiff flesh of the bread.

The sound of Maya letting the ceramic bowl strike the countertop after depositing half the blended mixture into the frying pan filtered him back into the soundscape of this reality. The sweet sizzling sound of a butter-drenched pan fixing the eggs whistled around his eardrums. He spoke, knowing what she had said without having to hear it and nearly cutting her off.

"I can't go see a shrink. What would I tell him? I'm having dreams about seeing a shrink back in the sixties?" Martin pulled a sardonic face, staring blankly at the wall before himself.

"There's nothing wrong with that, Martin . . ."

"Yeah right." Martin's tone drawled, oozing condescension with every word. "They'll think I'm completely whacko."

Martin's eyes crossed as he folded another piece of toast close to his face. The cracking surface shot tiny motes of burnt bread cascading down to the plate below. He began biting around it, carefully separating the crust from the crumb, consciously saving the folded area where the excess salty butter would be pooling for last.

"And what about the rest of it, huh Martin?"

The sizzling seemed to stop, and Maya's eyes were on the back of his head, intently probing the sharp, perfect angle at the back of his close-cropped hairline. The concentration he had on his toast didn't falter, even the sense of her penetrating gaze couldn't distract him.

"Lots of people have nightmares about the war, Martin . . . lots." She sounded slightly more exasperated this time, her pleading tone taking on a bitter air that was different. "And lots of them get help. There's nothing wrong with it. My father had to . . ."

She trailed off slowly as Martin's head lolled slightly, following the course of his rolling eyes as he prepared his usual rebuttal.

"Why do you have to keep comparing me to your father, huh?"

He turned now, his eyes blue flame towards her. His chest was heaving with a pent-up passion he hadn't realized was growing within him. The air froze between them, and their stares hung momentarily, each clambering for position. Each striving for domination. The sizzle of the pan returned, and Maya turned to mash her egg concoction, striking the pan with a fork.

"I'm not *comparing* you to my father," she said. "I'm only trying to help you out, okay?"

Silence again held the floor, that bitter temptress of conflict begging to be broken but needing to be upheld. Martin took another bite of his folded toast and mashed the bread as he spoke.

"Look . . . you can help me by leaving me the fuck alone," he said, succumbing to the temptation of conflict. "I've lived with this sort of thing my whole life, so it's not that big a deal, okay?"

The air bristled slightly beside Martin, and silence reigned supreme once again as time froze. What had been Maya's back—turned to him as she'd toiled over the stove—was suddenly her front, panting and red-faced, her breasts heaving against her pale blue shirt, and all at once the sharp spike of a ceramic bowl half-full of blended eggs shattered against the peach-coloured wall across the table from Martin. Tiny rivulets of the yellow paste began to form, threatening to run down the now scared surface as the fragmented pieces of the bowl clattered to the floor like spent casing. All the sound of the world returned again as Martin rose from his seat with determination. The ambient sound was different this time. It was heavier. Thicker. And much, much more electric.

His teeth gritted on the butter-soaked bread clenched between them, grinding sideways as salty fat splashed against the back of his now pulsing tongue. His eyes still saw Maya standing opposite him, the fork with which she'd been beating the eggs was in her hand like a weapon, her hair suddenly enflamed, and her body seemingly poised to strike, but he was already on top of her, pressing the small of her back into the sharp hard edge of the countertop. His left arm had her thin left wrist, the threat of the egg-soaked fork subdued, his right hand had gripped her along the jawline, thumb pressed deeply into her cheek, offsetting her jaw painfully.

No words, only silence between them. Only rage. Her free hand flailed, stopping at instances against the countertop, trying to support herself for fear that her back may snap. She could feel her spine succumbing to the counter. His breath was hot and hard against her face. Tears began welling up in the corners of her eyes and running down her high cheeks. Her jaw hurt so much. Her back hurt so much. Would her wrist break first though? Her mind could only repeat to itself that she didn't want to die, *she didn't want to die*, as her body began failing her, feeling as though it were tearing apart.

Martin's panting slowed, his rage seeming to subside slightly, and his pressure against her relaxed, but not his grip. She felt his hot breath receding, the demon in his soul crawled back down to its depths, and she let her muscles go slack. She could fight no longer, even if she wanted to. She fluttered her eyes, struggling to blink away the film of tears that blurred her vision, and their bodies together began winding down their sudden outbursts. Her mind relaxed, and she could think again, and realized his grip wasn't loosening. Before she could think why Martin pulled her up and away from the counter. His grip actually tightening, her left hand now pulsing in agony, and her teeth grinding painfully in her twisted jaw as he held her at half-arm's length before him.

"What the *fuck*?" he said through clenched teeth.

She hissed back through pursed lips, spittle firing at him through her uncontrollable mouth.

"You, Martin . . . you the fuck, that's what!" Her eyes grew wide, dark brown irises glaring at Martin. The pain was numbing now. "I've given up everything for you, Martin. Everything! I changed the course of my life, and for what?" Her jaw realigned as his hand softened its hold on her face. "To be shit on at your convenience? I care, Martin, that's why I do what I do. I care for you. Why else would I stay with you? But now . . . now . . ." The fork clattered to the tiles as she let it go, her body slacking again in his grip. "Now I'm tired, Martin. I'm tired of fighting. I'm tired of fighting for you. I'm tired of fighting with you. You do whatever the fuck you want to do, just don't expect me to be there with you! I've got my own problems. I don't need your problems too."

"It's *not* your problem, Maya . . ." Martin's tone was softer, his teeth still clenched, and his grip now more to hold her aloft than inflict pain.

"It *is* my problem, Martin!"

Her eyes flashed again, and Martin looked at himself. His outstretched arms, their grip on her body, her tear-stained face, crooked jaw, and his squarely planted feet, lowering his centre of gravity into a fighter's stance.

He released Maya, and a shiver ran through his limbs and surrounded his torso. His spine suddenly ached with the entirety of a lifetime of labour, and he slumped to the floor, his body lax. Slowly his limbs began to curl around him. Slowly he began to ball up. Alone on the floor in his own fetal embrace, Martin began to whimper.

8. Nightmare

His bed was cold, but he suffered it like she had suffered him. The thin sheets draped over him feigning warmth, providing a false cocoon for his larval self. If he loosened his jaw, he feared his teeth would chatter uncontrollably and send spasms throughout his body, and so he lay taught in the darkness. The cold inched its way into his flesh, arousing him and making it difficult to sleep, so he stood from his bed, naked, and peered through the slats of his blinds to the grey-stained twilight world outside.

The land rolled out from him in all directions, spilling forth in unending undulations of blackened moss-carpeted dunes. It was bordered on either side with jagged, craggy mountain peaks that seemed to touch the edge of the sky, but the earth ran away in front of him forever beyond the horizon. The horizontal prison bars of the blinds blurred into one another as the double-sealed windowpanes stretched away to nothingness. The acrid thickness of the air around him, burning, weighed into each pore as his unblinking eyes scanned the horizon like a lost predator searching for an unknown quarry.

A spark ignited in his mind, stabbing at the back of his vision, and caused him to blink. A man lay screaming, his cries that of a thousand men. He clutched at his left thigh, the rest of the leg a mangled and disfigured mess from the knee down. Crushed into the dirt, it was invisible, indiscernible from the earth, his deep crimson-brown blood clotted and indistinct against the clay-red earth. He opened his eyes, staring again at the endless sea of dead earth rolling before him.

Another spark, another blink, and a boy, eighteen at most, baby-faced and ghost-pale, was coughing up blood. Tar-black and thick, like molasses in late February, it poured down his weak chin and over the gaping hole in his chest. His entrails lay strewn before him like the long, crooked fingers of the devil, red and glistening in the night. His still-beating heart pounded vigorously in his chest cavity behind broken ribs, and with a final thump, he was back in the world of endless hills and impassable mountains. His breath caught in his throat as he inhaled deeply, and before another spike could stab at his synapses, he closed his eyes, exhaling with purpose, with intention.

He returned to that world of dying men. That world so real, yet so unbelievable. As he looked down at the wastes below him, he could see those men filled jagged trenches stretched across the landscape, splitting and cracking the land into sharp, tenuous sections. The thunderous clamour of gunpowder and subsequent rumble of each falling mortar betrayed the soldiers' shovels, destruction becoming the reason for the fractured ground. He could count the dead if he tried, each one a silently screaming soul before him.

One shot in the head. One in the arm. He blinked, but the ravaged countryside remained. Two were shot in the legs. One in the gut. Blinking again, more fervently this time, he opened his eyes on the horror still. Four of the men had their flesh wrenched from their bones by the backfiring of a mortar. Two. One. Blink. Nine. Five. Blink. Maybe he couldn't count them. Too many dying. Too many already dead.

He watched the vascular system of trenches fill up with men clambering over each other like rodents in a flooding cavern. On a signal lost to the din of war, they discharged, exploding from the ditch like blood from a sliced artery. A sheet of men ten deep, aged sixteen to twenty-six, sweeping across the ravished plain. And each of these men fell to the hard-packed mud that was once a lush, fertile field. They would sway momentarily as the wheat here once had in gentle breezes before falling to the farmer's scythe. This process continued, the dying body of war filling its veins with men and emptying them to their deaths over and over again.

The blood of the bodies, tens of thousands deep now, ran in streams from the battlefield to the trenches, eroding their way back in smooth trickling paths that grew steadily into raging rivers. The ichor ran heavy and fast, tidal waves of muddy blood crashing into the breakwater of the filling trenches until the soldiers could no longer line up and gather for their slaughter. The channels of men, choked off from their release forward and still pressed from behind, filled with the dark crimson blood, drowning them before they could die. These rivers of gore crisscrossed the tortured landscape, building new channels and reshaping the earth right before his eyes. They raced in all directions, turning back on themselves, braiding their way towards a common fault.

He saw the rivers of blood as they meandered from the horizon to his feet and, raising his hands to his face, found the blood was on him—seeping from empty eye sockets.

9. Toronto, 1996

Nicola awoke to the deep growl of thunder and a flash of light across his room that caused his mirror to reflect the ghosts of his dreams. His mother slid into the room.

"Nevaeh . . . Nevaeh?"

Her voice had a singsong quality as she searched for Nicola's long-dead sister. Nicola sat up on his elbows in his bed and looked about. What was he doing in his bed? His attention moved to the moon-coloured sheets draped over his lower half. He never slept in his bed. He glanced to the doorway that led to the small vestibule between this room and the living room. He preferred the rigidity of his couch, the one he had reinforced with plywood and two-by-fours.

This wasn't real. He must still be dreaming.

The spectre of his mother continued to search the room, looking for her daughter. For Nevaeh. She feigned opening drawers and looking behind the curtains with stone-faced disinterest. Nicola's eyes followed her movements about the room, his head dipping and bobbing as she slowly made her way about. Overlooking him, she peered under the bed with closed eyes, still chanting her daughter's name in relentless monotony. The swaying arcs of his head tracing her ghostly dance drew him from the bed as his movements began to mimic hers in a caricature of her graceful form.

His bare legs slid from their warm patch of mattress, passing between cold cotton sheets. He stood, unsteady on his feet, momentarily balancing in a light-headed haze as he stared at his pale, bony feet. Raising his head, he glanced around for her, his heart jumping momentarily, thinking he'd lost her—but there she was, near the door, turning away from the wardrobe towards him. He stepped forward, his feet unsteady still, like a toddler taking their first step, the world unfamiliar from this vantage point, the body unsteady as it attempted something new. His eyes remained transfixed on her, and while her form was well defined, he was still unable to see his mother's face. The last time he saw her, he'd had a similar issue. That was, of course, over forty years ago, one week after she had died. Then, as now, she was dressed in what appeared to be a wedding gown—but Nicola understood it as a large baptismal outfit, the proportions reimagined for an adult.

Finding his footing, Nicola slipped by his mother as she began her circuit of the room again, her calls for his lost sister fading into the distance. His steps felt as though they were floating along the slick parquet floor, appearing unblemished and unaged, as if newly refinished. Silently he slid through the doorway, left open by his mother's entrance, without interrupting her lament. As he crossed the threshold, he remembered that, over fifty years ago, the exact same thing happened. He saw his dead mother looking for his dead sister, and he left the room in silence, lost and looking for something, but not quite sure what.

The hallway felt colder than usual, but his body hardly noticed. On a conscious level, he knew he should be shivering, but his body felt oddly warm, heated evenly from the inside out. Slowly he padded the six careful steps that led to the entrance to the living room through the whitewashed wooden doorway, cautious for no clear reason. His wife was on her couch to his left, her face buried into the back of the velvety chesterfield, the thin yellow blanket covering her rising and falling slowly as she breathed. Her feet, poking out from beneath the bottom of the sheet, were covered in thick grey woolen socks. Looking past her, towards his couch, he found himself staring at his own body, lying there as usual, perfectly still.

He moved closer to himself as he lay there, appearing slightly contorted and awkward. He knew he shouldn't be able to see himself like that—like others see him, like a stranger to his own flesh. His face was oddly pale, his sunken cheeks more pronounced. It wasn't the face he was used to seeing in the mirror every morning. The grey stubble of his chin appeared to vanish into his white flesh, and his lips were slack, all the tension of his years seemingly released. He raised his prune-shriveled hands to his own face, as if touching it would reveal his true colour and shape. Then a knock came at the door. Turning and stepping toward the door, it opened before him of its own accord.

"I've been looking for something."

A blonde man in his sixties, or maybe fifties, faced Nicola across the threshold of his home. He was shirtless, wearing a pair of loose-fitting linen trousers that seemed to ripple of their own accord.

"Looking for a very long time," he said.

Maybe he was in his forties. Nicola squinted at him; it was so hard to tell one's age as you got older. Young people often mistook short periods of time for longer ones, so maybe he was in his thirties. The man wore a half-smirk on his face, not condescension but wry comprehension. Nicola opened his mouth to speak, dry yet soft lips parting for what felt like the first time, but the stranger continued.

"I didn't know what I was looking for. I couldn't remember what it was," he said. ". . . until I cleared my mind."

The smirk broadened ever so slightly into a smile. Nicola was puzzled as he stood there, staring at the stranger beyond his front door. He seemed to carry a presence that filled the whole of the outside world. He appeared so close and yet felt so far away.

"I was looking for you, Nicola."

The stranger's head nodded forward, vibrant blue eyes bugging open slightly as he indicated Nicola, standing before him in his own light, loose-fitting outfit.

"I've been looking, and waiting, for you for a very long time."

They stood in silence, the two men, eyes locked on one another's face but taking in the entirety of each other's presence. The man spoke again, serious but not grave.

"I've been waiting for you to die."

Nicola's body locked. The whole world seemed to collapse in on his mind as his eyes grew wide. His breathing stopped in his throat, panic rising in him, but unable to find purchase on his ethereal frame. He shot a glance back to his body lying on the couch in such a peaceful slumber. His face flushed of colour, paling him whiter than his own cadaver lying mere feet from him. As he turned back to the stranger, lips open in subdued awe, pupils dilated wide, the stranger held out his hand.

"Do I know . . . I mean, have we met before?" Nicola stammered out in Italian as his body moved of its own volition, gently reaching his hand out towards the stranger.

"Yes, we have, Nicola. But conditions were less than appropriate for introductions."

Taking a step backwards, the man dropped his hand from an upward palm of invitation to a welcoming handshake position.

"My name is Martin." Nicola's hand instinctively reacted, turning itself to meet Martin's in a hearty grasp. "Martin Engels."

"Piacere. My name is Nicola."

As their hands touched, Martin's subdued expression ascended to a full and gracious smile.

ܒܩܝܫܐ ܐܢܐ ܕܝܢܐ ܕܝܢܗܝ"

And as they both dissolved to nothing, a magnificent set of pearlescent-white wings spread tall and wide from Martin's back, the thick layers of feathery plumage occluding the world around them. With a swift beat of his wings, they were gone in an instant, leaving behind only husks:

Martin's corpse sprawled across a bed of blood-soaked satin sheets, his eyes wide and vacuous, a warm handgun clutched in his left hand; while Nicola's lay peacefully on his couch, the scowl of the weight of his life and times shrugged off his face for good. In the breast pocket of his plaid sleeping shirt was a note. Written in Martin's hand but bearing Nicola's signature.

Manufactured by Amazon.ca
Bolton, ON

35287503R00107